MR. RIGHT NOW

BAES OF JUNETEENTH

SHERYL LISTER

ABOUT MR. RIGHT NOW

When it comes to business, Mr. Black Los Angeles, Dante Powell believes in planning down to the smallest detail, and that includes the Juneteenth festival he's spearheading. His personal life is another matter, however. He lives by one simple rule - no strings, only flings. But he didn't count on the one night of explosive passion he shared with Jayana Cole or seeing her again.

A one-night stand. That's all it was supposed to be. Now, Jayana isn't sure it's all she wants. Yet mixing business with pleasure could put her job in jeopardy. But Dante is a temptation she can't resist, and she intends to show the die-hard bachelor that some rules are meant to be broken and she's his right now...and forever.

ACKNOWLEDGMENTS

My Heavenly Father, thank you for my life and for loving me better than I can love myself.

To my husband, Lance, you will always be my #1 hero!

To my children, family and friends, thank you for your continued support. I appreciate and love you!

To my anthology sisters, you ladies are amazing!

Thank you to all the readers who have supported and encouraged me. I couldn't do this without you.

DEAR READER

Dear Reader ~

I'm so excited to be a part of this anthology and I hope you enjoy Dante and Jayana's journey to finding love. I also hope you will be inspired to step out in some way to continue the fight for Black equality. As always, I look forward to hearing your

thoughts.

Love & Blessings!
Sheryl
sheryllister@gmail.com
www.sheryllister.com

THE UNTOLD LEGACIES:

MR. BLACK ORGANIZATION

Every legacy has a story ... this is ours.

Dante Powell steered his rental past the large Victorian that housed the African American Historical Museum and parked around back next to what looked like a storm shelter or old bunker. He got out, walked to the door and entered the code. Instead of taking the elevator, he opted for the stairs. Dante took in the cool, damp space with its metal railing, painted concrete walls and exposed piping. *This is where it all began.* Five Black men, including his grandfather, had come together at the height of the civil rights movement and founded the Mr. Black organization in an effort to bring hope to their communities across the nation. That legacy had been passed down to his father, and now him.

He stepped out into the otherwise silent hallway, the sound of his expensive loafers echoing on highly polished concrete floors. His steps slowed as he came upon the photos of the founding families lining the walls, pausing at one of his grandfather and a small smile curved his lips. Isaac

Powell, Sr. had brought Dante to this place shortly after his sixteenth birthday and a day after a fated visit with his high school guidance counselor. When he'd expressed a desire to become an electrical engineer, she'd given him a patronizing smile while suggesting he might be better off pursuing a sports career, since he was good at it, or something less challenging. He'd angrily pointed out his perfect grade point average, the fact that his father owned a tech company and held the same degree, then walked out. Later, seated around the table with his grandfather, father and other family members who had made it their mission to provide every opportunity to Black and brown people, his quiet rage turned into a raging passion to do the same. In his current role as Mr. Black Los Angeles, he planned to continue that pledge. He inhaled deeply and let it out slowly, then continued to the conference room. Inside, three pairs of eyes turned his way when he entered. "What's up?"

Preston Scott glanced down at his watch before extending his hand for a fist bump. "I can't believe you're late."

He always made it a practice to value other people's time and was rarely late. "Couldn't be helped. Flight was delayed." Dante greeted the other two men–Nero Bond and Titan Stone–the same way. "Where's Porter?" Porter Crowne rounded out the fifth member of their group and had a penchant for being late.

"You know his ass ain't never on time," Titan said.

He chuckled. "True that."

"How's the City of Angels?" Nero asked.

"Not that angelic." They caught up on each other's lives, then the conversation turned into a spirited discussion of sports.

Porter strolled in, impeccably dressed as always, and Dante shook his head.

"How's the youth center going?" Porter asked

"Better than I'd hoped. We just received two grants from private foundations and one from the city." All three would go a long way in funding their educational and artistic endeavors, as well as staffing.

"Let me know if you need anything." They did a fist bump and Porter continued greeting the others in the room.

"Okay, let's get started," Preston stated, interrupting the various conversations as he took out his tablet. "As part of the founding families, we've all been members of Mr. Black since we turned twenty-one. Yet, it wasn't until I was attending the networking event this past October that I realized for the first time since our grandfathers and great-grandfathers stood in this room, that each founding family has a member as the chosen Mr. Black rep for their city right now."

Dante's expression wasn't the only surprised one around the table.

Titan spoke up. "I suspected it had been a while, but I must have been so busy with work, I didn't realize this was the first time in over fifty years."

Dante had the same thought.

Preston leaned back in his chair. "I don't think the National Executive Board realizes it either."

"If they had, no doubt they would have called us into a private meeting at the event to try to figure out a way to rein us in," Dante added with a snort. His father had once told him that the board would try to tell him not to push too hard, to let things happen in their own time. At the same time, he encouraged him to push back when necessary and do the things that *felt* right.

"And I still can't get over the fact that none of the members of our family are sitting on the board right now," Nero said.

That opened up a conversation about their next steps. They had a prime opportunity to make an impact and he was here for all of it. Dante clasped Porter on his shoulder. "Luckily, as founding families, we have clout in this organization even without any of our family on the board."

"We have our forefathers to thank for that," Porter said.

Preston nodded. "We do. But I'm more concerned about using our leverage in our cities since up until now, all five of us weren't in this role."

"What were you thinking?" Nero asked.

"Juneteenth is now a federal holiday, but it doesn't change the fact that most of the nation is not even acknowledging it," he answered. "Nor do many Black folks even know why Juneteenth is important."

"You want us to be more educationally focused." Titan said. "Be more aggressive in our approach to teach our cities through Mr. Black about our culture."

"And shed a bigger spotlight on our history," Dante finished.

"You both read my mind," Preston mentioned.

"Because my mind was there too," Dante responded. It had been one of the reasons he'd opened the youth center. The five of them tossed out ideas with the intention of focusing their Juneteenth celebrations toward the youth, to encourage them to set their sights higher, and to not accept inequality and inferiority as a way of life.

The meeting continued, and as it had become their custom, Porter pulled out his special bottle of imported whiskey and placed three shots in front of each of them. Dante tossed back the first shot for his father and grandfather, the second one for the two friends he'd lost to gun violence, and the third wasn't to drink, but to be poured onto the concrete floor in memory of their fallen brothers and sisters around the world.

The passionate discussion continued, the deep bond between them strengthening. That they all had been voted in at the same time wasn't coincidence. In his mind, it was destiny. Their destiny. *His* destiny. They had four months. It was time to kick ass and they were just the men to do it.

PROLOGUE

"You know all we can ever share is right now," Dante Powell said to the half-naked woman standing in his hotel room.

A sultry smile curved her lips. She unhooked her bra and let it drop to the floor, then slowly slid the tiny matching purple panties down and off her long, toned legs.

She sauntered over to where he still stood leaning against the door, transfixed by her smooth cocoa skin. His gaze made a slow tour down her body—full breasts and a narrow waist that flared out to generous hips. A jolt of lust went straight to his groin and he felt his erection getting harder by the second.

Sliding her palms up his chest, she wound her arms around his neck. "Okay, Mr. Right Now, let me see what you've got. We don't have a lot of time."

In the blink of an eye, Dante's clothes hit the floor. Yes, their time was short, as she had a connecting flight later, but for some reason, he didn't want to rush. He wanted to take his time touching and kissing every part of her curvy body. Pushing the thought aside, he reached for his discarded pants, retrieved a condom and rolled it on. "Then we'd better get started. Right here." He lifted her in his arms, turned and placed her against the nearest wall.

She wrapped her legs around his waist. "Mmm, I like the way you think."

Their eyes connected and he felt a spark of...*something*. Instead of dwelling on it, he captured her mouth in a hungry kiss. She moaned, fueling his desire even more. Her head fell back and he trailed kisses along her jaw, exposed neck and back up to reclaim her lips. Dante gently sucked on her tongue while slowly gyrating his lower body to the same rhythm. He reached between them, circled her clit with the pad of his thumb, and slid first, one finger, then a second one inside her.

She shuddered. "Oh, yes. Right there."

He dipped his head and latched onto an erect nipple. She cried out. He sucked and licked until her body trembled, then lavished the same sweet torture on the other one. Dante felt the tiny contractions and knew she was close, but he wanted to be inside her when she came and withdrew his fingers. She whimpered. "Don't worry, baby. I've got you." He eased his shaft inside her until he was embedded deep within. His eyes closed and he didn't move for several seconds, relishing in her tightness surrounding him. He began moving, plunging deep and retreating in a slow, erotic cadence that sent heat spiraling through him. She moaned and arched her back. He kept up the pace, each stroke going deeper and deeper. Dante planted his feet and increased his movements.

"Don't stop," she panted.

"I don't plan to, not until we're both satisfied," he murmured, moving faster. He grabbed her hips and guided her to move faster. Her hands dug into his shoulders and her inner muscles clenched him tight. Dante could feel himself teetering on the brink of his control, but he wasn't ready for it to end. His body trembled slightly and he closed his eyes as the sensations intensified. "Damn, girl," he said, pulling her into a passionate kiss.

Abruptly, she broke off the kiss and let out a scream as she climaxed all around him. He tightened his hold on her hips, drove into her faster and moments later, he went rigid, threw his head back and exploded. Dante let out a low groan as his eyes slammed shut.

She rested her head on his shoulder, their breathing ragged. "This was the best layover I've ever had."

Dante chuckled softly, aftershocks still wracking his body. The touch of her hand on his face made him open his eyes. She kissed him with a sweetness that went straight to his soul, shocking him in the process. For a brief moment, he fantasized about them getting together again. Then he remembered what happened the last time he let a woman get close to him and dismissed the notion. One night. That's all they could ever share. That's all he'd ever want from a woman.

CHAPTER 1

"*A*re you ready for the summer rush?"

Dante glanced up from signing the papers on his desk and nodded at his best friend and business partner, Ryan Hendricks. "Enrollment is up by about twenty-five percent from last year." The original Impressions youth center, run by another friend, Bryson Montgomery, had prompted Dante to open Impressions 2 Community Center three years ago. They'd met when his tech company donated laptops. Later, he volunteered and enjoyed it so much that he wanted to do the same, providing more children with a safe place to learn and grow. The after-school and preschool programs ran year-round, and they opened full-time in the summer.

"Then it's a good thing we hired those two new teacher assistants." Ryan leaned back in the chair and crossed an ankle over his knee. "That reminds me, the new counselor starts today. Man, she is *fine*," he added with a grin.

"The only thing we need to be worried about is her doing her job." They'd had to fire the previous one after some of the students complained about the woman's lack of empathy.

The last straw came when the woman told a student with body image issues to start hanging around people closer to her level of physical attractiveness or make some uglier friends. Dante had fired her on the spot, but it had taken more than three weeks to get the teen back on track. He just hoped the new person had more compassion. Ryan mentioned her being closer to their age—in her mid-thirties—so he'd keep his fingers crossed things would work out. "I'll meet with her after the staff meeting."

"Then you can see up close that she's exactly your type."

"What is it with you? You've been trying to hook me up with one woman after another for the past couple of months. I don't want to be hooked up. I like my life the way it is. Besides, running the center and the tech company doesn't leave much time for anything else." Along with the youth center, Dante served as CEO of the tech company his father started. Thinking of his father made his chest tighten. It had been four years since his father's death and the pain of losing his hero felt as sharp now as it did then. Forcing the emotions aside, he turned toward his computer and opened his emails.

Ryan stood, stretched and headed for the door. "You aren't getting any younger and it's time to let go of the past. And before you start spouting the same bullshit about you have, let me remind you that over the past four years, whenever you've taken a woman out, it's one date and done." He paused. "*If* you bother to take one out at all. You can lie to yourself, but I've known you for thirty-two of your thirty-seven years, my brother, and what you're doing isn't healthy. Maybe you need to be the first one to make an appointment with the new counselor. See you in the conference room for the meeting." Ryan walked out.

Dante dragged a hand down his face. He had no desire to be in an exclusive relationship. He'd tried that once, had even proposed, but in the end, her betrayal had taken something from him that he couldn't get back. *Never again.* Straightening in his chair, he went back to his emails.

"Morning, big brother. You're holding up the meeting again."

His head came up sharply. "Hey, Erika. What did you say?"

Erika pointed to the clock on the wall. "The staff meeting. Everybody's waiting for you." She frowned. "Are you okay? You've been really distracted for the past month or so."

"I'm fine," he answered, pushing to his feet. He'd lost track of time answering emails pertaining to both the center and the tech company. He grabbed the folder containing the meeting agenda, a notepad and pen and headed for the door.

Erika folded her arms and blocked his path. "Something's going on with you, Dante. Ryan noticed it, too. It started right after you came back from that trip to Dallas." She narrowed her eyes. "Did something happen with the new tech deal?"

Dante sighed. Times like these almost made him regret bringing his best friend and little sister on board. Ryan was bad enough, but Erika—six years his junior—acted as if she had as much right to his personal business as he did. Yeah, something happened. A lot happened, but none of it had to do with the company or the new deal he'd been working to finalize. "Everything with the deal is progressing and there's nothing going on," he said instead. He lifted a brow and gestured toward the door. "Do you mind? We don't want to keep everyone waiting."

She moved aside. "I'm going to find out sooner or later."

"There's nothing to find out." He shook his head and left her standing in the doorway as he headed to the conference room at the end of the hallway. "Good morning," he said to the six people seated around the table as he claimed the chair at the end. "Sorry about being a little late. I lost track of time." Erika took the empty seat next to his and, still glaring at him, set a huge mug on the table. She lived on coffee and needed two or three cups to get her going. "Okay, let's get started. School will be out for the summer in four weeks and that means we'll be going back to our full day hours of eight to five-thirty."

"Oh joy," one of the teachers said, eliciting a round of laughter. "Are we doing the camping trip again with Bryson and his crew?"

"We are, and it'll be the first weekend in June, as usual, but I may not—" Dante paused when the receptionist stuck her head in the door.

"Sorry to interrupt, but the new counselor is here." She stepped back.

It can't be. Yet, there she stood, as if she'd walked out of his dreams. Dante forgot to breathe. He didn't even realize he was on his feet until he heard Ryan clear his throat. Shaking himself, he crossed the room and extended his hand. "Welcome to Impressions 2. I'm Dante Powell." Her smile hit him squarely in the chest, the same way it had the day they met.

"I'm Jayana Cole. It's nice to meet you." She gave his hand a little squeeze before releasing it.

Erika and Ryan stared with raised eyebrows, but Dante ignored them and gestured Jayana to an empty chair and made the introduction. *Jayana.* He liked the name. And her. "We can meet one-on-one after this meeting and I'll catch you up."

She nodded and sent another knowing smile his way.

He tried to recall what he'd been talking about before Jayana came in, but for the life of him had no clue. "What were we discussing?"

"We were talking about the camping trip," his sister said with a smirk.

"Oh, right. I may not be able to go since I'm heading up the Juneteenth festival this year."

Ryan chuckled. "One of your Mr. Black Los Angeles duties."

Dante shot his friend a look. While he loved giving back and working with the kids, he preferred keeping a low profile, something he found difficult in his new role. He would hold the position for four years before someone new was selected. "Moving on." Again, one glance at Jayana and he promptly lost his train of thought. "Um…I'll touch base with Bryson sometime this week to get the details and let you all know at the next staff meeting. Any questions?" When no one spoke up, he moved on to the preschool and the new teacher assistants.

"How many students do you typically have during the summer?" Jayana asked.

"Anywhere from forty to sixty-five." Once again, Dante couldn't stop staring at her. He whipped his head around and smothered a groan when Erika kicked him under the table.

"Someone else is asking you a question."

His eyebrows knitted together and he scanned the faces, wondering who'd asked. *I am losing it.* "I'm sorry."

"I wanted to know if the camping supplies we ordered had come in."

"Not yet, but I think the tracking says they should arrive by the end of the week." He went over the remaining items and ended the meeting. Less than two minutes after he got back to his office, Ryan and Erika barged in and closed the door.

"Man, what the hell is wrong with you?" Ryan asked. "And did I miss something with you and Jayana?"

Erika dropped down in one of the chairs across from his desk and crossed a leg over the other. "I was going to ask the same thing. You could barely get through the meeting."

Dante waved her off and stared out the window, which overlooked the center's playground. "I don't know what you're talking about," he lied. From the moment Jayana strutted into the room, the heated memories of their brief time together played like a loop in his mind, messing with his self-control. He rarely got caught off guard, but today his sister was on point. Of course, he had no intentions of telling her that, though. She didn't need another reason to be in his personal business.

"Oh, please. You stumbled through that meeting like a drunk on his fifth shot of whiskey."

Ryan burst out laughing. "She's got a point. So, you might as well tell us the real deal, especially now that she's an employee."

The fact that Jayana was now employed by the center and by default, him, should have been enough to make sure things remained professional. *I won't ever let myself be vulnerable to another woman again* he kept repeating to himself. However, the sexy grin she shot his way, along with the attraction still simmering between them let Dante know it might not be so easy. He braced his hands on the window sill and closed his eyes. From her thick curly mass of brown hair streaked with golden highlights and sparkling dark eyes set in an exquisite cocoa face, to her full breasts that fit perfectly in his hands and the way her feminine muscles clenched around his—.

"*Dante!*"

Erika's voice cut into his sensual thoughts. "What?" Glancing over his shoulder, he met both Erika's and Ryan's curious gazes. Sighing, he said, "I know her. I mean, I met her a few weeks ago on the flight to Dallas."

A slow grin curved Erika's lips. "Well, now. I *knew* it. *She's* who has you so distracted."

A knock sounded on his door and Ryan got up to open it. "Come on in, Jayana."

Jayana entered the room fully and paused. "I'm sorry. I didn't realize you were in a meeting."

Erika stood. "We're not, and we're leaving." She turned toward Dante and mouthed, "We aren't done with this conversation."

Dante ignored her.

"I'll catch up with you later, D," Ryan said as he exited behind Erika and closed the door.

Jayana smiled. "Well, if it isn't Mr. Right Now. Didn't think I'd ever see you again."

"Same." And that made her a safe choice. He gestured to one of the chairs. "Please have a seat."

Instead of immediately moving, she asked, "So how have you been?"

"Good. You?"

"Same. Surprised, but in a good way. Seeing you has me wondering about another round of *right now*."

He had the same thought, and so did his body, if the speed at which it reacted to her words was any indication. From the moment she'd slid her shapely backside past him to take the window seat on the plane, then said, "Hmph, so this is how the other half lives. I may have to travel first class more often," he'd been intrigued. So much so that when her connecting flight had gotten canceled and the next available one was six hours later, he'd invited her to a late lunch. They'd laughed, talked, and ended up in his hotel room having the best sex of his life. "It can't happen again."

She chuckled as her gaze slowly traveled over him. Closing the distance between them, she stopped just short of touching him, but close enough for him to feel the heat rising and smell the lingering notes of the sweet, sensual fragrance she wore. "Then you should probably make that clear to certain parts of your body." With a bold wink, Jayana slid into the chair.

Dante couldn't say one word. His body and mind were definitely on opposite tracks, and although it wouldn't be easy, he was going to do his damnedest to overrule his body.

Jayana Cole stared at the man who had been starring in her nightly dreams for over a month. Surprise didn't come close to how she felt when she walked into the room and saw him. He'd been dressed in a suit when she met him on the plane and she thought he looked good then—a little over six feet, toffee skin, a textured high-top fade, jaw-hugging beard, and a diamond stud in his ear that gave him a bad-boy edge. Seeing him now in the well-worn jeans and black tee that molded against his well-defined upper body, she couldn't decide which she liked better. For someone who sat behind a desk, the man's body was a work of art. They sat silently, his dark, piercing eyes boring into hers with the same intensity as the evening they spent together. Only this time, she sensed his struggle, as if he was battling between what one wanted to do versus what one should do. The attraction was still simmering and she knew it wouldn't take much for it to be rekindled.

"So, tell me about this place," Jayana said, breaking the sensual spell. "I'm surprised you weren't the person to interview me, especially since we ended up on the same flight."

A slight grin kicked up in the corner of Dante's mouth. "I usually do conduct the interviews, but I had a meeting that couldn't be rescheduled. As far as this place," Dante waved a hand around, "we opened the doors three years ago."

She listened as he told her about their preschool, after-school and summer programs. The passion with which he spoke added even more intrigue. Not many men would give their time to a program like Impressions 2. "I'm really impressed."

"Thanks. Do you have any questions?"

"Actually, I have a few. First, what made you decide to do this, and what did you do before?"

"I love kids," Dante said. "After volunteering at the original Impressions, run by a buddy of mine, I figured we could help more kids with a second center. We do our best to support their well-being and promote activities that will help them develop skills—educational, emotional, assist them in recognizing their capabilities and worth. We want them to feel comfortable trying new things and have to confidence to take risks, understanding that failure is more like a step toward progress, rather than a sign to give up."

Jayana nodded. "I think I'm going to enjoy working here. May I ask what happened to the last counselor?" His jaw tightened, but he didn't respond immediately. "I'm not trying to be nosy, I just want to be aware of anything that has negatively affected the students, so I can determine the best course to take."

"You're fine. Let's just say she lacked the compassion needed to deal with the students and, more than once, talked down to them."

She felt her anger rise. "Why in the world would she venture into the world of counseling without having empathy? That makes no sense. She could've ruined somebody's life doing some mess like that." Jayana clamped her mouth shut. The man probably thought she was crazy, going off on her tangent. In her defense, she despised psychologists who did nothing more than offer a couple of platitudes, then collect their fee. "Sorry about that," she said sheepishly.

"Don't apologize. Your passion is admirable and shows

you care. It's just what we need. Anything else you need to know?"

"During the interview, Ryan mentioned something about you needing my assistance with a Juneteenth festival. Is this what you were referring to in the meeting earlier?"

"Yes. So far, I've secured the park, some of the food vendors, and the music, but I still have a list of those who haven't responded that we'll need to follow up with sometime this week. I don't want to wait until the last minute. Still working on a theme and some other activities."

"Okay. I'll put my thinking cap on and see if I can come up with something. One last question. How did you become Mr. Black Los Angeles?" She'd googled it after the meeting and saw that the Mr. Black organization honored Black culture, Black love and Black history. They had chapters all over the country.

Dante ran a hand over his beard. "Someone nominated me, I was chosen. End of story."

One thing she recalled about him was that he didn't talk much. Not that a whole lot of words were exchanged once they made it to his hotel room. Jayana stood and headed for the door. "Well, I think you're a good choice. It says that their men are bold, loyal, ambitious, cool, and king." She loved the play on the acronym for black. Her hand paused on the doorknob. "It fits you perfectly, especially since I googled you too and found that not only do you run this center, but you're also the CEO of InstaGenix." And on both sites, his photo was nowhere to be found. "How do you have time to run both companies?"

"I'm fortunate enough to have a great person running the day-to-day operations there, freeing me to be here most of the time."

She nodded. "One last question."

"What's that?"

"Why isn't your photo on either website?"

"Because neither the tech company nor this center is about me."

It was refreshing to meet a man who seemed to leave his ego at the door. Unlike her sorry ex-boyfriend. "I can get with that. See you later."

Back in her office, Jayana spent much of the afternoon going through the files of the students who had been counseled and found the information sorely lacking, and in a few cases, non-existent. The students had been documented as attending the session, however there were no corresponding notes for some of the days. She sighed heavily, closed the file and tossed it on her desk. Just as she reached for another one, a knock sounded on her partially open door. "Come in." She smiled when Erika walked in.

"Hey, Jayana. Are you settling in okay?"

"I am. Have a seat." Whereas she stood five-seven in her bare feet, Erika was a good three or four inches shorter and wore her hair in an elaborate braided updo. She'd met the woman briefly when Jayana had flown in for the interview.

Erika leaned forward and asked conspiratorially, "So, how long do you need to work here before I can ask what's going on between you and my brother?"

She burst out laughing. "Oh, my goodness. I think we're going to get along great." Jayana was pretty outgoing and most often spoke her mind, and she sensed with Erika's question, she might be the same way. The only thing that surprised her was that they were siblings. However, as she studied the woman, who looked to be about her age, she could see the resemblance. "There isn't a whole lot going on. I met him on my flight home after the interview." She kept the details to herself.

"Mmm hmm. With the way you two were sneaking those heated looks at each other during the meeting, I was afraid y'all would set the room on fire. I've never seen him look at a woman the way he did with you this morning." She stood and angled her head thoughtfully. "I know there's more. I also know Dante is going to try to put the brakes on anything that might develop. Don't let him. You'll be good for him. I love him and he deserves to be happy," she added softly. "Let me know if you need anything."

Still trying to process Erika's last statement, Jayana nodded. Once the door closed, she leaned back in her chair. *What did that mean?* So lost in her thoughts, it took a moment for her to realize her cellphone was buzzing. Snatching it up, she smiled upon seeing Karina Hall's name on the display. The two had been best friends since ninth grade. "Hey, girl. What's up?"

"That's what I called to ask you. So, how's the first day going?"

"It's actually going pretty well. I had a chance to introduce myself to a few of the teens and hang out in the preschool. If all goes well, it would be a dream job—less stress, no long hours."

Karina's laughter came through the phone. "Then you'll have plenty of time to look for that sexy brother you had layover sex with. Man, I wish stuff like that would happen to me. Every time I fly, I end up sitting next to someone as old as my grandparents, or who talks incessantly about nothing I'm interested in hearing, then drops off and starts snoring."

Jayana laughed so hard, she had tears. "I'm so glad we're going to be in the same city again. I've missed this." Karina's company had transferred her from their hometown of Atlanta to Los Angeles a year ago. She had been the one to let Jayana know about the job notice at Impressions. "And I won't have to go far to find him." There was complete silence and she glanced at the display to see if the call had dropped. "Karina?"

"Wait. What...what does that mean?"

Smiling, she said, "It means that he's founder of this youth center."

"You. Have. *Got* to be kidding me!" Karina screamed with excitement. "Oh, shoot. You're going to get me in trouble. I'm sitting at my desk."

"Me? Nobody told you to scream."

"Hey, I wasn't ready for that little announcement."

With the way you two were sneaking those heated looks at each other during the meeting, I was afraid y'all would set the room on fire. She hadn't been ready, either. Not for the intense chemistry that still burned between them. Not for the strange emotions that had bubbled up. Not the fact that, despite agreeing to a one-night-stand weeks ago, seeing him again made her want to pick up where they left off.

CHAPTER 2

*F*riday afternoon, Dante stared out his office window at Jayana laughing with a group of teen girls. He marveled at how well all the kids had taken to her in the week that she'd been there. In just a few short days, she'd found a way to bond with the students in a way that the former counselor hadn't been able to do in more than a year. Initially, he'd had some concern about Jayana working at the center, not because he didn't think she couldn't do the job—he trusted Ryan's judgement. His problem was purely personal. She made him feel and want things he'd promised to steer clear of, and no matter how hard he tried, he couldn't erase her memory from his brain. Now, seeing her every day made it even harder. To her credit, she hadn't mentioned anything about them indulging in *another round of right now* since their conversation that first day, but the teasing sparkle in her dark brown eyes had kept him fantasizing and dreaming about the same thing. Dante had taken more cold showers in the past five days than he had in four years. No other woman had ever kept him tied in knots the way Jayana did, and he didn't understand why. He'd never had a problem moving on from a woman, and he had yet to figure out what made her different.

"Obviously, you don't have anything to do if you have time to just stand around staring out the window."

Dante barely acknowledged Ryan, and continued to focus on the scene on the playground. Jayana now had her head thrown back and he could almost hear her lyrical laughter and the passionate sounds she made as he'd kissed his way from her mouth, neck and shoulder. Ryan came and stand beside him, and he reined in his thoughts.

"Ah, I see now."

"You see what?"

"Everything you refuse to see. The reason I've been standing in your office for a good three minutes and you've yet to say one word. Jayana is a beautiful woman—tall, curves for days, and all that gorgeous hair. Makes a man seriously consider wanting to change his single status."

Dante stiffened. The thought of his best friend with her sent a streak of anger through him.

Ryan chuckled. "That's what I thought."

He shifted his gaze to Ryan. "What are you talking about?"

"Jayana. You want her. Don't bother denying it because I've caught you staring at her more than once since she started working here. I said what I said to get a rise out of you, and the way your body just tensed up proves I'm right. If she has you this tied up in a week, what do you think it's going to be like in a month or two?"

"Nothing's going to happen." The lie sounded hollow in his own ears. He was a heartbeat away from dragging her into his office and taking her up on her offer. And he had the perfect wall. "She's an employee, remember?"

"We don't have any written rules about dating, and it definitely wouldn't apply in your case since the two of you hooked up before she started working here."

That thought had crossed his mind, as well. However, Dante knew one more time wouldn't be enough with Jayana. Everything about her screamed *relationship*, despite claiming that she wanted nothing more than an afternoon of good sex. "I never said we hooked up."

Ryan gave Dante a look that said, *don't insult my intelligence*, then folded his arms, as if waiting for Dante's confession.

Sighing, he shoved his hands in his pant pockets and turned toward the window again. "It was only once. I finally figured out it was the same day she interviewed here. We ended up on the same flight to Dallas."

"I was already impressed by her, but she just moved up a few notches. Any woman who can stay on your mind for longer than it takes me to finish my dinner has to be special."

He laughed softly at Ryan's wacky humor. "I don't know how I put up with you all these years."

Ryan snorted. "I don't know how I put up with *you,* with your nerdy ass. If it wasn't for me, you'd still be trying to figure out how to even *talk* to women."

Dante just shook his head. "Shut the hell up." Whereas Dante fell somewhere on the ambivert scale with a tilt toward the introverted side, Ryan was a straight up extrovert and had nearly every girl in the school fighting for his attention. Dante, on the other hand, preferred to date one girl, and had for almost two years until their post-graduation endeavors took them in different directions Neither had wanted to deal with the hassle of juggling a long-distance relationship and college courses, and had parted amicably. The same couldn't be said about the next two women he'd dated. Both had been into drama, definitely not his style. But it was his most recent ex, who'd made him decide to discard any notions of marriage and the proverbial happily-ever-after.

"Seriously though, bro. Your self-imposed exile has gone on long enough." Ryan gestured toward the now empty playground. "I have a feeling Jayana might be the perfect woman to help you get back out there. If you need some pointers, I got you," he added, clapping Dante on the shoulder.

He shrugged the hand off. "Shouldn't you be working on securing a few more grants?" Ryan handled the center's finances.

"I'm handling my business *and* making time to play. You should do the same." He glanced down at his watch. "It's after five, and I'm taking off. How late do you plan to be here?"

"Probably another hour or so. I have a few things to do for the Juneteenth festival." All the vendors had been secured, but he wanted to add a youth-focused piece and wasn't quite sure what he wanted to do yet.

Ryan nodded. "Let me know if you need me to do anything."

"Mom wanted to know if you were coming to Erika's birthday dinner tomorrow evening."

Ryan rubbed his hands together and a huge grin spread across his face. "You'd better believe it. I will *never* turn down a meal prepared by Mama Daphne."

Dante smiled. The first time he'd invited Ryan over to dinner in second grade, Ryan had praised his mother's cooking. Going forward, he found every reason to stop by during dinner, and still did.

Erika stuck her head in the door. "Hey, guys. All the kids and teachers are gone, so I'm leaving. Don't be here all night," she added, her gaze focused on Dante.

"I'm on my way out too, so I'll walk you to your car," Ryan said. "Later, bro."

"See you at Mom's tomorrow." Dante crossed the room and kissed his sister's cheek. "Drive safely, sis."

"I will." She pointed two fingers toward her eyes, then toward Dante. "I meant what I said." She did it once more for emphasis. "I'm watching you."

Smiling, he said, "Girl, go home. I'll be out of here no later than six-thirty."

Erika rolled her eyes, then said to Ryan. "He acts like we don't know him."

Laughing, Ryan slung an affectionate arm around her shoulders. "You have a point. We're out."

Dante chuckled and threw up a wave as they exited, then went back to his desk. He opened the festival file on his computer and before he could start, a knock sounded on the door. Without looking away, he said, "Aren't you supposed to be gone?"

"Um, I was on my way out and saw your light on."

His head snapped around and he slowly rose to his feet. "Jayana. I thought you already left for the day."

Jayana leaned against the doorframe with her arms folded and one foot crossed over the other. "Nope. Still here. You have a few minutes?"

He nodded and waved her in. "Sure." He leaned a hip against the edge of the desk. "What do you need?" He realized what he'd said as soon as the words left his mouth.

Her eyebrow lifted. "Loaded question. How about we save it for another time?"

Dante couldn't do anything but smile. "You are something else."

She dropped down into one of the chairs next to him. "Yeah, I know. But what I actually came to talk to you about was the festival. You mentioned wanting to have a youth-focused activity and I have an idea. What about renting the California African American Museum and hosting a private party for the kids and their parents? I looked it up and it says they can open their galleries. After talking with some of the students here, I got the sense that not very many of them have ever had the opportunity to attend a black tie type event."

The passion in her voice matched his and he found himself captivated by both the idea and her. "I like it, and I agree." The museum had a collection of art, history and culture, all with an emphasis on California and the western United States. "Dinner, a program with a short talk about the history of Juneteenth, museum tour—"

"A band and dancing," Jayana finished.

Dante's gaze zeroed in on her lips and he had to force himself to focus on the conversation. "I think it's doable and exactly the type of event I'd envisioned, but the majority of these kids live at or below the poverty line."

She waved a hand. "We can figure out how to get them fancy outfits, but for now I took the liberty of reaching out to the museum and, surprisingly, no one had booked it. I guess people are focusing more on other ways to celebrate. I hope I haven't overstepped. I figured if you didn't want to do it, I could always cancel. I just didn't want to chance someone snapping it up over the weekend."

"No, no. I appreciate the initiative." Outside of his founding Mr. Black brothers, he hadn't found anyone else with the same determination. Her excitement sparked his own and he'd do everything in his power to make it a night the students and their parents would never forget.

Jayana stood. "Great. I'll get out of your way."

Straightening from the desk, he asked, "Any plans for the weekend?"

"Not much. Just hanging out with my best friend, and doing more unpacking."

Dante didn't know why he felt so relieved by the fact that

she hadn't mentioned a date. "Hopefully, you don't have much left to do."

She shook her head. "Just a few more boxes."

He knew he should stop talking and let her leave, but for some reason, he wanted her to stay. He searched his mind for another topic, but nothing came. Instead, their gazes locked and the air thickened around them. Dante tried to force himself to take a step back, but found himself moving closer. Seconds ticked off and he realized he was fighting a losing battle. "Jayana."

Jayana placed a finger on his lips. "Don't talk. Just kiss me."

His mouth swooped down on hers before she finished her sentence good. He took his time reacquainting himself with the sweet taste of her kiss. And just like last time, he couldn't get enough. She slid her hand up his chest, then down again and cupped him through his jeans, sending a sharp jolt of pleasure through him. Dante muttered a curse and abruptly broke off the kiss. He was *not* supposed to kiss her again, but somehow, his common sense took a hike whenever she turned those big, beautiful brown eyes on him. Breathing harshly, he stared down at her. "This was not—"

"Yeah, I know. It wasn't supposed to happen again, but I'm honest enough to accept that there's something happening between us." She backed out of his arms. "Let me know when you're ready to do the same." Leaning up, she brushed a soft kiss over his lips. "Have a good weekend, Dante." She strode out of the office without waiting for his reply.

She'd thrown down the gauntlet. But was he ready to pick it up?

∽

"Oh, my goodness! I'm so glad to see you," Karina said, hugging Jayana. "Come on in, girl." They'd seen each other only once since Karina moved, and that had been almost six months ago.

Jayana entered the two-bedroom Carson condo located less than ten minutes from her own. She scanned the open layout. "I like this. And did I thank you for hooking me up with the job and the condo?" When Jayana accepted the position at Impressions 2, Karina had emailed the listing for three condos near hers that were for sale. Thankfully, because she'd gotten a good price for her previous condo and accumulated a decent amount in her savings, she'd been able to secure a two-bedroom, two-bath in another complex by the same builder.

Karina laughed as she led Jayana to the kitchen. "Only about a thousand times. We can talk while we eat."

"Well, I'm grateful. It was the easiest move I've ever made." She took in the small foil-covered plates lining the counter. "Whatever is under these smells so good, and I'm starving."

"I know how much you love seafood, so I did some different appetizers," she said as she removed the covers to reveal mini crabcakes, bacon-wrapped shrimp, lobster bites and fried salmon bites, along with raw vegetables and spinach dip with sliced baguette.

"And this is why you're my best friend. I'm going to enjoy every bite." Her friend had gone out of her way to prepare some of Jayana's favorite foods. She placed some of everything on a plate and carried it over to the kitchen table, then waited for Karina to do the same.

Karina went back for sangria, filled two glasses and placed the pitcher in the center of the table.

After the first bite of the crispy, seasoned salmon, she

moaned. "Oh, this is *so* good. You know I'm going to need the recipe."

She smiled. "I got you, girl. Speaking of moving, has Calvin tried calling you again?"

Jayana rolled her eyes at the mention of her ex. Since their breakup, he'd called almost weekly begging for a reconciliation, but she wasn't biting. "Not since the week before I moved, and I made sure not to mention it. He wanted to know why I hadn't called him. I asked him why he thought I would since we'd broken up over three months ago. And it wasn't like we parted on good terms."

Karina paused with her glass halfway to her mouth and she shook her head. "That fool is seriously not playing with a full deck. I'm so glad you kicked his crazy behind to the curb."

"Me, too." Crazy didn't begin to describe Calvin. The first couple of months in their relationship had been fine, but he increasingly seemed to unravel right before her eyes and his emotional immaturity became more and more pronounced. She'd tried to talk to him, suggest he see a therapist—someone other than her—and be patient. However, his stark denial that he had a problem had forced her to end things to protect her own wellbeing.

"The new guy you're dating sounds like he's the complete opposite."

She frowned. "I'm not dating anyone. Who are you talking about?"

"You know, your boss." Karina scooped some spinach dip onto a slice of the baguette and took a bite.

"Girl, we aren't dating. As a matter of fact, Dante said nothing could happen between us." She finished chewing a lobster bite that nearly melted in her mouth before continuing. "I mean, we're still attracted to each other, but...." She shrugged. His sister's words came back to her. *I love him and he deserves to be happy.* Had something transpired in his past that kept him from pursuing relationships? Part of her wanted to seek out Erika to clarify, but the other part said she should leave it alone. Yet, after the kiss they shared in his office last night, she was even more curious.

"I'd love to be a fly on the wall to see how that turns out. If you two didn't have to see each other every day, I could see it fizzling out. Being front and center forty hours a week is going to make that a little challenging."

"Challenging doesn't begin to describe it," Jayana murmured.

Karina narrowed her gaze. "What are you not telling me?"

She told her friend about their first conversation on Monday, the heated looks and ended with last night's kiss. "It's like he's conflicted and can't decide what he wants to do. His sister said something that makes me think whatever is going on with him is tied to his past. Even she picked up on the vibes between us and came right out and asked me about it."

"Hold up. His sister works there?"

"Yep and is a straight trip." Jayana took a sip of her drink, then told Karina about the rest of the conversation.

"You know, she sounds a little like you. You've never had a problem saying what's on your mind."

She thought about it for a moment. Erika did strike her as a person who, like her, got right to the heart of a matter. In Jayana's mind, it left little room for misunderstandings. "You're probably right. She's cool people, though."

"Back to Dante. Do you like him?"

Jayana shrugged. "So far. He seems like a really good guy, and you should see him with the kids. Most people who run these kind of non-profits stay in their offices. Not Dante. He talks to them, plays basketball, helps them on the computer."

Karina lifted her glass in a mock toast. "And he's fine and can bring it in the bedroom."

She smiled. "The icing on the cake." After being with him, her definition of "great" sex completely changed. The brother had touched, kissed and licked every part of her body, and the sex was off-the-charts amazing. His kisses had nearly melted her on the spot. Even now, she could almost feel the slow, sensual way his tongue curled around hers. Reining in her thoughts, she took a huge gulp of the sangria, hoping to cool off.

"What do you plan to do?"

"There's not a lot I can do if he's not on board. I did tell him to let me know when he's ready to accept that there was something growing between us."

"Again, straight-to-the-point," Karina said with a chuckle. "Maybe, he'll come around."

"Maybe, maybe not. When we met, I was cool with just the one time because I thought I'd never see him again. Now, I don't know if I want to have that kind of relationship with him, knowing we have to see each other every day. Does that make sense?"

"It makes perfect sense. You and I always talked about finding that one and having the kind of relationship our parents do. There's nothing wrong with holding out for what you want. I sure am."

Jayana agreed, but had no idea whether that man would be Dante.

CHAPTER 3

*D*ante arrived at his parent's home early Sunday afternoon. He'd promised to help with the meal preparations. Rather than another big party like she'd had for her thirtieth birthday last year, Erika had requested a family dinner instead. He let himself inside and found his mother in the kitchen humming along to an up tempo jazz song. Leaning in the doorway, he watched her for a moment before making his presence known.

He wrapped an arm around her waist and kissed her cheek. "Hey, Mom."

She startled and brought a hand to her chest. "Dante. Boy, you almost gave me a heart attack sneaking up on me like that." She swatted him on the arm.

Grinning, he said, "Sorry. You were so into your music, you obviously didn't hear the door opening." He took her hand, swung her out and moved in time with the beat. She loved music and dancing, and he could recall many times when she and his dad would spontaneously dance anytime of the day or night. He'd wanted to have the same thing, but now didn't hold out hope. An image of Jayana's smiling face surfaced in his mind along with her bold statement. That he was attracted to everything about her was a given, but he still didn't know if he could let down his guard enough to allow anyone near his heart again.

"You're dancing, but I can tell something's on your mind, son," his mother said, cutting into his thoughts. She stopped and peered up into his face, studying him as only a mother could. "Is everything okay?"

"Yep. Just have a lot to do at the center and for the Juneteenth festival next month." Dante washed his hands in the sink and dried them on a paper towel.

"Oh, that's right. I remember you mentioning you were heading that up. Do you need my help with anything? I can get some of my sorority sisters to pitch in."

"Not right now, but I'll definitely let you know." Daphne Powell was a retired educator, but spent much of her time serving the community with her beloved Alpha Kappa Alpha sorority. "What are we having?"

Going back to the sink where she was cleaning up the remnants of collard greens, she said, "Your sister asked for grilled steaks, macaroni and cheese, greens, candied yams, hot water cornbread and strawberry shortcake for dessert."

He smiled. "It probably would've been easier to list what she *didn't* ask for. I'll handle the steaks and slice the potatoes. Not touching the mac and cheese or the cornbread. Nobody makes it like you."

His mother angled her head in his direction. "Are you trying to butter me up for something?"

Dante let out a short bark of laughter. "No. I'm just telling the truth. Besides, I'm sure Erika's going to ask whether you made them." His sister did not play about her coffee or her food. He removed the steaks from the refrigerator to season them.

She chuckled. "You're right. That child has always been particular about her favorite foods. Is Ryan coming?"

"Of course. You know he never turns down a free meal, especially one of yours. And now that his parents moved to Arizona, you probably won't be able to get rid of him."

Putting the now cut greens into a pot, his mother said, "Well, he's always been like another son to me, so he's welcome anytime. So, any new prospects for a daughter-in-law?"

"Aw, Mom, don't start." For the first couple of years after his break-up, she'd given him space. However, for the past six months, she'd renewed her efforts to get him down the aisle.

"Don't start what? You're thirty-seven years old, Dante. Closer to thirty-eight, if I'm counting. The way you're going, you'll be taking your child to daycare on a cane and I'll be long gone."

Ouch! "Tell me how you really feel," Dante muttered as he sliced the yams.

"I am. Aren't you listening? You can't tell me there's not one woman who you'd like to spend some time getting to know better. Someone who'd make a good wife."

"I tried that once and remember how it turned out?" He hated revisiting that time, the feeling of helplessness, the loss. Bracing his hands on the counter, he bowed his head and closed his eyes to staunch the flood of emotions threatening to engulf him.

His mother came and placed a comforting hand on his back. "Baby, you've got to let go."

"I don't—" Dante stopped mid-sentence when he heard his sister's voice and quickly schooled his features. The last thing he wanted was for her to worry about him on her special day.

"Mom, I'm here!" Erika bounced into the kitchen with a wide smile.

"Happy birthday, sis." He lifted her off her feet and swung her around like he'd done when she was little and planted a kiss on her cheek.

"Thanks, big brother. Hi, Mom." She hugged their mother. "Ooh, it smells so good in here. You didn't let Dante make the mac and cheese, right?"

Dante and his mother shared a look and burst out laughing. He said, "I told you she was going to ask. And no, I didn't touch it. I'm on steak and potato duty."

"Then I'm going to be eating good because your steaks are melt-in-your-mouth-slap-yo-mama *amazing*. But I'm not talking about slapping you, Mom," she added hastily.

Their mother gave Erika's shoulders an affectionate squeeze. "Oh, I know. I've said that phrase a time or two, myself. I'd better get back to cooking if we want to have dinner on time. You get a pass for today, so I suggest you take it."

Erika held up both hands. "Say no more. I'm going to recline on the deck. Let me know when dinner is ready." She headed for the sliding glass door on the other side of the kitchen. "Oh, and I like my steak with just a hint of pink."

"I know how you eat your steak," Dante said, waving her off.

He and his mother finished cooking while discussing his ideas for both Juneteenth celebrations. Ryan arrived just as they finished and he went to let him in.

"What's up, bro?" Ryan said as he entered and pulled Dante into a one-arm hug. "Man, it smells good in here and I'm starving."

"Then you should've come earlier to help. Always showing up after all the work is done."

"Hey, I know my place, and it ain't near a stove." They both burst out laughing. Ryan could cook some basic foods, but relied mostly on meal services, ordering out or showing up at Dante's house. He followed Dante to the kitchen. "Hey, Mama Daphne."

A smile blossomed on her face and she spread her arms wide. "Ryan. How are you, baby?"

"I'm good," he said, hugging her. "You're looking as beautiful as ever."

She giggled like a schoolgirl and Dante shook his head. His friend hadn't changed since grade school.

Ryan glanced around. "Where's Erika? I saw her car in the driveway."

"She's on the deck, lounging like she's Cleopatra," his mother answered. "Tell her to come in so we can eat."

"Okay."

While Ryan handled that task, Dante and his mother brought everything to the dining room table.

"Happy birthday to me," Erika sang, Stevie Wonder style, when she entered the dining room.

They settled around the table and after his mother blessed the food, filled their plates and dug in. Dante smiled at Erika when she pretended to swoon after eating a bite of the steak. Seeing his baby sister's happy face as she ate chased away the blues that had grabbed him earlier.

"Mama Daphne, you put your foot in this mac and cheese," Ryan said. "If I promise to mow your lawn every week and wash dishes, can I get dinner say three times a week?"

His mother's soft laughter floated across the table. "I'll see what I can do."

He grinned at Dante and Dante said, "You really need to learn how to cook and stop begging."

"Hey, there's no need when Mama Daphne rules the kitchen." That brought on more laughter and old stories.

Halfway through the meal, Erika said, "Mom, I think Dante might have a new girlfriend."

Dante choked on his iced tea and he shot a glare at his sister.

His mother whipped her head in his direction. "Is that right? Why didn't you tell me when I asked earlier?"

"Because I do not have a new girlfriend. Erika's just being the same bratty little sister she always been."

"Her name is Jayana and she's the center's new psychologist," his sister continued as if he hadn't spoken.

"Hmm, I may have to stop by sometime next week and meet her. Maybe you should invite her to our next family dinner."

Dante's heart started pounding in alarm. *Invite her to dinner?* That's how it started with his ex and there would not be a repeat.

"She's a beautiful woman," Ryan said with a smirk, the same one his sister wore on her face. "And the kids really seem to like her."

Dante wanted to strangle them both, and toyed with returning his sister's gift *after* he told her what she would have gotten. But he knew he wouldn't. He loved her, even if she was a pain in the butt. Deciding to steer the conversation away from him, Dante said, "A few of the girls mentioned the same thing to me."

"That's good. I didn't think Maureen was the right person for the job," his mother said as she dabbed the napkin against the corners of her mouth. "I've heard nothing but good things about her when she worked at the hospital, but it takes someone special to work with children."

With three pairs of eyes still on him, he said, "I agree. I think she'll be a good fit for the center." *She might be a good fit for you, too, if you let go of the past.* Dante finally admitted to himself that the more he was around Jayana, the more he wanted to get to know her. But doing that meant opening himself up to possibility of falling for her, something he wasn't ready to do.

Jayana spent the first half of the week meeting individually with all the students who attended the center on a regular basis. She planned to add a couple of group sessions per week, as well, but wanted to wait until school let out so she'd have an accurate number. Leaning back in her chair, she smiled. So far, this had been the best job she'd had, hands down. Everyone, from the staff to the students, had welcomed her and treated her as if she were family. One of the preschool teachers had even given her a small welcome basket filled with a mug, assortment of teas, cookies and chocolate.

The only person she hadn't seen was Dante. They'd communicated by email about the festival details and other things pertaining to her job, but he kept his distance. Jayana tried not to let it bother her, but for reasons she didn't want to analyze it did. Standing, she did a few stretches to relieve some of the kinks from sitting at her desk for the past hour. The center would close in about twenty minutes and only a handful of students remained. Her plans for the evening included dinner, bingeing the last few episodes of S.W.A.T. and taking a long bubble bath.

"Ms. Cole?"

Jayana turned and saw four students congregated in her doorway. "Hey. Come on in. What can I help you with?"

"We keep hearing Mr. Powell and everybody talking about Juneteenth but we don't know what it is," Travis said. He tended to be the outspoken one in the group.

"Have a seat and we can talk a little before your parents get here." Instead of sitting behind her desk, she sat with them in the area she'd reconfigured that had comfortable chairs arranged in a circle. "Juneteenth was originally cele-brated in Texas, when the enslaved were finally told they were free. The thing is, it was over two years after President Lincoln had signed the Emancipation Proclamation freeing them."

"That's whack. What took so long for them to find out?"

"Let's just say those in power decided to keep the free labor going," she answered. Jayana opened her mouth to say something else, but went still when Dante appeared. "Hey. Come join us."

"I don't want to interrupt your session," Dante said.

She stood and patted the chair she'd vacated. "It's not a session. They're asking about Juneteenth. You can sit here."

The students called out, "Yeah, come on, Mr. Powell," and "We want you to come in."

Dante smiled and took the seat she offered.

"Ms. Cole told us it took two years for Texas to find out slavery was over," Travis said. "Then they started the celebra-tion called Juneteenth."

"Did they do Juneteenth in LA, too?" Kira, another student asked.

Dante shook his head. "Not initially. Here in LA, they celebrated Emancipation Day, usually on New Year's Day. One of the earliest documented celebrations was listed in the Los Angeles Herald in, I think 1874 on New Year's Eve. That year they had a dinner and dance. There wasn't a huge African American population here at that time, so most of the gatherings were centered around the church and featured speeches from former slaves. It wasn't until a large number of people, as part of the Great Migration, came to Southern California from Texas did Juneteenth become popular."

Jayana didn't know who was more captivated as he spoke, her or the students. Dante's knowledge about LA's Black history had her wanting to grab a notebook and pen to take notes.

The receptionist stuck her head in the door. "So this is where you all are. Your parents are here, guys."

A chorus of "aww" sounded.

Dante stood. "You'll be back tomorrow, so we have plenty of time to talk. But it might be better if you researched it on your own in the computer room," he added. He gave each student a fist bump as they trudged out, clearly not ready to leave.

After a round of goodbyes, only Jayana and Dante remained in the office. Jayana said, "That was amazing. I felt like I was in class. You really should think about teaching."

He chuckled. "Nah, I'll leave that to the real educators. You weren't too bad yourself."

"I love talking with them. They ask about a million questions, but they're great kids and I know they're going to go far."

"That's the reason I started this program. I want them to have every opportunity to succeed in whatever career they decide."

They stood staring at each other for a lengthy moment. "So did you need to talk to me about something?"

"Just wanted to check on you, see how things are going, and find out if you needed anything."

"No complaints so far."

"I'm glad to hear it. Are you planning to stay late tonight?"

Jayana smiled and went to her desk to start packing up. "Nope. I'm actually leaving on time. What about you?"

"Same. Would you like to go out to dinner?"

She paused placing her laptop in her tote. "As in a date?"

The corner of his mouth kicked up. "You can call it that if you like."

A part of her was ready to shout, *hell yeah!* But the

conversation she'd had with herself and with Karina about wanting more from a relationship made her hesitate. She angled her head. "Is this about you wanting another night of sex?"

Dante chuckled. "I'd be lying if I said the possibility of sharing another night of passion with you hasn't crossed my mind, but no. That's not what this is about. Last week you told me to let you know when I was ready to accept that there's something going on between us." He shrugged. "I want to get to know you, Jayana. That's all. For now, anyway. I can't promise that I won't kiss you, though."

"That's good because I kind of like your kisses. And I'd love to have dinner with you. What do you have a taste for?"

His brow lifted. "You keep asking questions like that and dinner will be the last thing I *taste*."

Jayana resisted the urge to fan herself. It took everything in her not to tell him he was free to taste any place he wanted. The look in his eyes and the slow grin that spread across his face said he knew exactly what she'd been thinking. "Okay, so not the best choice of words. I'll save them for later...when we know each other better." She slung her tote on her shoulder. "Tonight, will be dinner and conversation."

Still chuckling, Dante said, "I like you, Jayana Cole."

"Ditto, Mr. Right Now." She slapped a hand over her mouth. "My bad. That's supposed to be for another time." She lifted one finger. "Lemme just tip on out this office before I get into more trouble."

He threw his head back and roared with laughter. "Yeah. Good idea."

They were still laughing as the locked up and headed out to her car. Jayana asked, "Should I follow you?"

"No. We'll drop your car off at home first and take mine."

Her gaze went to the late model Audi parked a few feet away. "Nice ride." She wanted to argue that it would be a waste of gas, but the look on his face let her know it would be a waste of time. Besides, it was nice to be out with a man who exhibited just a little chivalry for a change. "Okay. I live in Carson." That had been another perk of her new job. It only took fifteen minutes to get to the center located in Gardena. Back home in Atlanta, her commute took forty-five minutes, on average.

He held the car door open and waited for her to get in. "I'll be right behind you, so try not to be a speed demon and lose me on the road."

"And miss out on a date with you? Please, I'll be driving as slow as molasses."

Dante shook his head and smiled. "I see this is going to be an interesting evening."

His smile made her pulse skip. "Interesting is good. Beats a boring date any day of the week." She wiggled her fingers in a little wave. "See you in a few." *Let's see if you're really ready for me, Mr. Powell.*

CHAPTER 4

*D*ante had made reservations at Fleming's Steakhouse in El Segundo before asking Jayana out. Fortunately, she'd said yes. He hadn't done anything this impulsive since…never. She had him so outside his comfort zone, he didn't know if he was coming or going. After handing the car off to valet, he escorted her up the steps and into the restaurant where he gave his name to the hostess.

"It's pretty crowded in here," Jayana whispered. "Hopefully, the wait won't be too long."

"We shouldn't have to wait at all, since I made reservations."

She glanced up at him. "Before or after asking me out?"

Dante hesitated briefly, studying her and trying to determine what she might be thinking. But her expression gave away nothing, which probably served her well in her profession. "Before. I figured I could always cancel if you said no, but I didn't want to take the chance of us having a long wait." Some women would think it presumptuous of him, but he considered it planning.

"I like a man with a plan," Jayana said, echoing his thoughts.

Before he could respond, the hostess called his name and showed them to a booth. She handed them each a large black folio containing the menu, then departed with a smile.

She opened the menu. "I've never been here. What's good?"

"Depends on what you like." When a teasing smile blossomed on her face, he realized what he'd said. "Food. We're talking about food," he said.

Jayana stared at him innocently. "That's what I'm talking about."

Dante laughed softly. "Uh huh." Her easygoing personality was one more thing on a growing list that drew her to him.

"Have you tried the scallops?"

"I have, as well as the lobster tails, and they're both good. I'm guessing you like seafood."

"You guessed right."

He loved seafood, as well, and wondered what else they had in common. A young man appeared at the table to take their drink order.

"I'd like a pineapple lemon drop," Jayana said.

"And I'll take a brown sugar old fashion."

"I'll be back with those drinks shortly," the young man said.

Jayana touched Dante's hand. "I'm ready to order if you are."

"I'm ready." They both opted for seafood—lobster for him, scallops for her—and shared sides of Fleming's potatoes and roasted asparagus.

"Thanks for dinner," she said when they were alone again. "I didn't expect all this." She waved a hand around. "I would've been fine with a good burger or pastrami sandwich."

"I know the perfect spot for both, so we can go there next time, if you like."

She wiggled her eyebrows. "I like."

Dante couldn't stop the smile that spread across his face. His family and Ryan often accused him of being too serious, but he didn't seem to have that problem when he was around Jayana. He'd smiled and laughed more with her in the past week and a half than he had in two months.

"So, I'm really excited about the different things you've put together for the festival and the dinner. And Erika told me you're adding two more teaching assistants at the center. You've built a great place."

"We did and I hope things turn out well with the celebration." Dante leaned forward, picked up her hand and placed a kiss in the center of her palm. "But tonight we're not talking about the center, Juneteenth, or our jobs. Just us getting to know each other. We can discuss the other things tomorrow during office hours."

"I can't believe a guy like you isn't already married," she said. "This must really be La-La land since these women here haven't snapped you up."

He chuckled inwardly at her use of Los Angeles' old nickname, but didn't immediately respond, especially since the jury was still out on whether he wanted to be "snapped up." Finally, he said, "How do you know I'm not the problem?"

She angled her head thoughtfully. "Are you?"

The server returned with their drinks and Dante waited until he walked away to continue. "I have my faults just like anybody else." In his mind, his biggest one was trusting a woman who claimed to love him. He heard his mother's voice in his head, telling him *baby, you've got to let go.* Until now he hadn't even entertained the possibility of pursuing another woman, but this woman made him want to dip his toes into the dating waters again. Even still, he planned to proceed with caution.

"We all do," Jayana said with a little laugh. "But from what I've observed so far, they aren't serious or bad enough to make a woman run in the other direction."

"I can say the same about you. There has to be something wrong with the men in Atlanta." She was intelligent, giving and beautiful inside and out. Jayana took a sip of her drink, then darted out her tongue to lick off some of the sugar rimming the edge of the glass. The sight sent a sharp jolt to his groin. He tore his gaze away from her lips and refocused on what she was saying.

"I don't know if it's all of them, but there was definitely something wrong with the one I dated," she said with a mirthless chuckle.

After taking a sip of his own, he asked, "Care to elaborate?"

"Let's just say he was emotionally immature. He needed to be the center of attention *always*, everything was always someone else's fault, and he had a habit of yelling whenever he couldn't get his way."

Dante could hear traces of pain in her voice and it made him want to find the man and kick his ass. "How long were you together?"

"Almost six months. The first three or four months were fine, then it was like he flipped a light switch and the real him appeared. I suggested he talk to someone, but of course, he denied anything was wrong. So, I left to protect my own emotional well-being. Did it put me off of relationships for a while? Sure. But I decided I can't let one bad boyfriend control how I live the rest of my life."

Sort of like you're doing, an inner voice chimed. But no one died as a result, he argued as the familiar pain rose again.

Thankfully, the server returned with their meals, sparing him from having to respond. As they ate, he decided to turn the conversation to safer topics. "What do you do when you're not working?"

"Spa days, putting together Lego sets."

"Lego sets?" he asked with surprise.

"Yes, but not those ten dollar kid ones. The ones I like are for adults, have far more pieces and the price tag to go with it. They have everything from the Eiffel Tower and Rome's Colosseum to the Titanic and themes from the Marvel movies. So far, I've done Black Panther and the infinity gauntlet."

"You'll have to show them to me sometime. I don't know what I expected you to say, but playing with Legos never crossed my mind."

"It's relaxing and you should try it. I also love journaling and taking long walks on the beach. With this warmer weather, I'm looking forward to going soon."

Another thing they had in common. For as long as he could remember, the beach had been one of Dante's favorite places. The smell of the ocean and the sound of the waves crashing against the shore had always given him a feeling of peace. It had been one of the reasons he'd purchased a home less than three miles away. "There are several to choose from here."

"Are you willing to be my tour guide?"

"Anytime you want." The words left his mouth before his brain processed them. He was supposed to be taking this thing slow. First the offer to take her to his favorite burger joint, now the beach. If he wasn't careful, he'd be promising to take her on a weekender by the end of the night.

Jayana finished the last bite of food on her plate. "That was so good. Thanks, again."

"You're welcome."

"You know, I've done most of the sharing tonight. You're not a big talker, are you? I'm going on and on, while you're throwing out these one-sentence answers. I notice you tend to sit and listen a lot more."

This woman had no problems reading him, and he didn't know how it made him feel, particularly because she'd described him to a tee. Dante preferred listening because, most times, he found that people will reveal who they are when you let them talk. Although, his ex had hid it well until that ring hit her finger. Being more of an introvert didn't help, either. His family, Ryan and a few other close friends were the only ones who he allowed to see his playful side. However, since they were supposed to be getting to know each other, he told her about his love of the beach, how he enjoyed running and playing basketball with the kids at the center. He also shared that he played the piano. His parents had insisted that he and his sister learn to play an instrument because of the connection between music and the brain. It helped with memory, cognitive function, and mood, among other things.

Her eyes lit up. "Oh, my goodness. You have to play for me one day."

"Sure." The excitement in her voice had him ready to say he'd play for her every day for the rest of his life. *Whoa, whoa, whoa! Rest of my life?* Dante needed to slow down. Deciding that he'd shared enough for one evening, he asked, "Would you like dessert?"

"No, thanks. I'm so full, I can't eat another bite. But if you want to order some, please do."

The dessert he craved wasn't on the menu, but he shoved the notion aside and signaled for the bill. After paying, he retrieved his car from valet and drove her back to her condo. Once there, he got out and went around to help her.

Jayana leaned up and kissed his cheek. "You're such a gentleman. I'm sure your father is really proud of you."

Dante went still at the mention of his father. She must have noticed because she stared up at him with concern.

She placed a hand on his chest. "What is it, Dante?"

"My father passed away four years ago."

"I am so sorry. Please accept my condolences. I didn't mean to bring up sad memories."

"I'm good." Yet, he knew he lied. He hadn't been good since the day he'd found his father lying in the middle of the floor of his parent's bedroom. Between her caring look and comforting hand still moving up and down his chest, it took all his effort not to bolt. She was slowly tearing down his walls and he couldn't find a way to make it stop.

Jayana nodded. "Would you like to come in for a minute?"

"Yes. You promised to show me your Marvel Lego collection."

"Oh, yeah."

He waited while she unlocked the door, then followed her inside and down a short entryway into a spacious living room.

Dante scanned the room. She'd decorated the room in shades of blue and gray, and whatever scent that filled the room made the space feel warm and inviting. "I like your place. How many bedrooms?"

"Two, which is perfect for me." She walked over to a bookcase on the far side of the room and gestured with a flourish. "What do you think?" she asked of the Lego designs she'd placed on one of the shelves.

He followed and carefully lifted each piece and studied it with an engineer's eye. The intricate design had him contemplating finding the nearest Lego store and purchasing one of his own. "This really isn't for kids. It's cool, though. How many pieces are in the Black Panther?"

"Almost three thousand. It took me a while to finish it."

"I might have to buy one." He placed them back on the shelf. "If I do, will you help me put it together?"

"Anytime you want," she said, throwing his words back at him.

"What I want right now," Dante said, easing her closer, "is to kiss you again."

"I want the same thing."

That's all he needed to hear. Before he could move, she pulled his head down and fused her mouth against his. Her tongue tangled with his, curling around it, gently sucking and driving him out of his mind. He groaned deep in his throat. His hands charted a path down her back and hips, then beneath her shirt to caress her silky skin. He reacquainted himself with every curve and felt himself growing harder by the second. Nothing about the kiss fell in the category of *taking things slow*. Everything in Dante's mind shouted for him to stop this dangerous road he was traveling, but he couldn't. Finally, he lifted his head. Their eyes held and a strange sensation stirred in his chest. He pushed it aside, reminding himself that he might be getting in too deep. What started as a one-time-only proposition was quickly morphing into something else. Jayana had turned out to be more than he expected. He'd never met a woman like her and he suspected he never would.

CHAPTER 5

*D*ante had a mountain of paperwork that needed his attention, yet he hadn't been able to concentrate all day. It had been over two weeks since their dinner date and Jayana dominated the space in his mind day and night. They'd shared a few kisses after hours, but hadn't spent time together due their schedules. From her smile and dark, sparkling eyes to her giving spirit, she made it difficult not to fall for her. On Monday, he'd arrived to find a small gift-wrapped box on his desk with a note that read, *Engineers need their favorite pen.* She'd purchased three of them, all stemming from a passing conversation they'd had about him needing to buy more because the ink was almost gone in his current one. This morning, she'd left another note: *A little birdie told me this was your favorite candy bar.* A gift bag with half dozen Snickers bars accompanied it.

Ryan and Erika had nothing but good things to say about her, and both had come outright and told him to get his shit together and make Jayana his. Even some of the teens had picked up on the attraction and thought it would be cool for Ms. Cole to be Dante's girlfriend. The only person who hadn't weighed in was his mother, and he knew without a doubt she'd be Team Jayana, especially since he knew his sister had been providing a play-by-play. Not only did Jayana fit right in with the two outspoken women in his family, but she'd done something no other woman had done in four years—make him want to try this thing called love again. A knock on his door drew him out of his musings.

Dante stood, rounded the desk and greeted his friend. "What's up, Big B?" Bryson eclipsed Dante's six-two height by a good two or three inches.

"I can't believe you're bailing out of going camping this year," Bryson said, pulling Dante in to a one-arm hug. "Out here being Mr. Black and dissing us little people."

He laughed. "You're acting like I'm sending my kids without any chaperones. Ryan and Erika are going, as well as the two teachers and four assistants. And you know a few of the parents have signed on."

"True, but you know I'm never going to let an opportunity to pass without throwing in that Black Organization."

Dante grinned. "Don't hate." He gestured Bryson to a chair. "Speaking of the Juneteenth festival, you're coming, right?"

"We'll be there. And thanks for the invite to the gala. You should've seen the kids' faces when I told them, especially the part about them getting their formal wear provided for free."

"That's what this is about." He'd reached out to a few shops that provide formal wear and four of them promised to provide the dresses and tuxedos for the students and their parents. "What brings you by on a Friday afternoon? I figured you'd be trying to get home to your wife and the twins. How are they doing?"

"Raven is good. She's actually been offered the lead physical therapist position at the rehab center where she works. Of course, she hasn't decided whether she'll accept it because it'll mean more paperwork. And the one thing my wife hates is paperwork," he added with a chuckle.

"Give her my congratulations. I ain't mad at her, though." His hand swept over the stacks of files on his desk. "I'd rather skip all this, too."

"Same, my brother. But I wouldn't trade what we're doing for the teens in our community. As far as the twins, Bryse and Gia are getting into everything, and I do mean *everything*. Explain to me how a couple of three-year-olds can get into a cellphone and download a bunch of apps."

Dante burst out laughing, but a pang of envy hit him. He thought he'd have one or two children of his own by now. "These kids are born tech-smart."

"Man, tell me about it," he grumbled. Thank goodness they all were free." Bryson spent a few more minutes sharing the antics of his twins.

"Oh, so you two are in here having all the fun and didn't tell me?" Ryan said, entering the office and exchanging a fist bump with Bryson. "I didn't know you were coming by today."

"I just stopped by to tease my boy about backing out of the camping trip, and was telling him about my wild twins." He shared the stories again, which brought on another round laughter. Bryson then asked, "When are you two going to get started? You're not getting any younger."

Dante shot him a dark glare. "You sound like my mother."

Ryan held up his hands in mock surrender. "Hey, I'm working on it. So stay tuned."

"What happened to that woman you were dating a few months ago? The one you brought to our Black history program."

Ryan blew out a long breath and scrubbed a hand across his forehead. "Man, we broke up a few days after that event. She complained the entire night about one thing or another

—the room was too cold, the food didn't taste fresh, the music was too loud and ghetto. I was two seconds away from putting her in an Uber so I could enjoy myself. I don't have time for that kind of bougie drama in my life."

Bryson laughed. "I'm so glad to be out of the dating game. What about you, Dante? You haven't dated anyone since that mess with Danielle, and that was four years ago."

Just the mention of her name spiked Dante's anger. "Unlike Ryan, I'm not trying to look for a woman."

"He doesn't have to," Ryan cut in, "She found him."

Bryson whipped his head in Dante's direction. "You holding out on me, old man?"

"Old, my ass," Dante said. "We're the same age. And I'm not holding out on anything."

Two quick taps on the door sounded. "Dante, I—. Oh, I'm so sorry. I'll come back later."

He was on his feet before he knew it. "We're not having a meeting. Come on in. I want to introduce you to Bryson Montgomery. Bryse, this is Jayana Cole, our new psychologist and counselor."

Bryson stood and extended his hand. "It's a pleasure to meet you, Ms. Cole."

Jayana smiled. "Jayana, please, and it's very nice to meet you, too. I've heard lots of good things about you and your center. I think what you and Dante are doing for our Black and brown children is amazing. I know it's making a huge difference in their lives."

"Thanks, and call me Bryson." I haven't heard much about you, but I'm sure I will." He turned toward Dante with a knowing grin.

"She's been here less than a month and the kids already love her," Ryan said.

She laughed softly. "Thanks for the vote of confidence, Ryan." To Dante she said, "I just wanted to let you know I'm leaving a little early today. I want to pick up the journals I ordered for the students."

"Be sure to give the receipt to Ryan so you can be reimbursed."

Jayana waved him off. "It's just a few little journals. Save that money for something else more important. I'll see you guys on Monday. Bryson, again, nice meeting you."

"Same here. I'm sure we'll see each other again since we partner on a number or activities."

"Sounds good." She threw up a wave and rushed out.

"I like her." Bryson reclaimed his seat and said to Dante, "So, how far gone are you?"

Ryan roared with laughter.

"Far enough." Dante didn't even bother to deny it. He was so far gone, he'd need a map to find his way back.

"Let me give you a little piece of advice. I know what happened all those years ago with Danielle hurt you, but you can't punish Jayana for something she had no part in. You know my story. Raven and I didn't have it easy either because of some past hurts and fears. And although our journey wasn't the easiest, every single moment with her has been the happiest in my life. It's worth every risk you'll take, Dante."

Hours later, after he'd gone home, he still couldn't get Bryson's words out of his thoughts. Raven had been holding on to her past hurts the same way Dante was doing now. But the last time he'd seen her, she'd been radiant with joy and the love between her and Bryson had been palpable. Dante stepped out onto the balcony in his bedroom and braced his forearms against the railing. His emotions had never been this out of control over a woman. Even his ex. He'd loved her, but those feelings didn't come close to the way he was beginning to feel about Jayana. *She's not Danielle.* And he couldn't see her doing the same thing that Danielle had done. Jayana didn't have a selfish bone in her body, and she'd proven it once again that afternoon with purchasing the journals. After one of her sessions related to using journaling as a way to get their thoughts and emotions out, a few of the teens expressed wanting to try it. And being the giving woman she was, took it and ran. She'd made their lives better already.

And she'd made his better.

Going back inside, he picked up his cell and sent her text: *What are your plans for tomorrow?*

Five minutes later, she replied: *I have a date with my laundry, but nothing else. You have something in mind?*

Dante: *Yes. I thought we could spend the day together.*

Jayana: *As long as it includes food and fun, count me in!*

He chuckled, and replied: *There will be plenty of both. I'll pick you up at noon, if that's okay.*

Jayana: *I'll be ready.*

He knew exactly where he wanted to take her.

Jayana stuck in her earbud and switched to hands-free as she moved around the room packing a small bag for her day with Dante. "I have no idea what we're doing. He only said we would have fun and to bring a change of clothes."

"See, this is where you and I differ," Karina said. "I would've asked a million questions about where we're going and how long we'd be there."

She laughed. "I've done the same a time or two with past dates, but I trust Dante. And I want to be with him."

"Girl, you sound like you're falling in love with the man. You've only known him for a month, I mean if you don't count that first hot encounter."

Jayana remained silent because her friend was spot on.

She'd asked herself countless times if she'd lost her mind. She *was* falling in love with Dante.

"Okay, Jay. You're quiet, and that tells me I'm right."

She zipped the bag and dropped down on the side of the bed. "Yeah, you are. He's so different in a good way and he makes me feel like... I don't know. I can't explain it." He wasn't a big talker, and they didn't need to fill every moment with words. Yet it was comfortable, peaceful, almost serene, and she didn't want to give that up. Or his kisses. "We're seeing where this leads, but what if it doesn't work out? I love being at the center and don't want to jeopardize my job." For her, that was the only drawback in pursuing the relationship.

Karina's sigh came through the line. "I hear you, sis. But you said yourself that he's a great guy, and I can't see him firing you if the relationship goes south. Impressions 2 is his baby and those kids need you. I promise he won't risk messing that up. Will it be awkward? Of course. But you both are adults and should be able to handle whatever happens as such."

"I know, and you're right." Dante had told her more than once that he appreciated the work she was doing with the students, and that he could see positive changes in some of them already. Her doorbell rang. "Oh, shoot. I have to go, Rina. Dante's here." She headed to the front.

"Alright. I'll be waiting on all the details of this mysterious date. Have fun."

"I will." Jayana disconnected, stuck the phone in her pocket and snatched out her buds. She glanced through the peephole just to confirm, then opened the door. "Well, hello handsome."

Dante bent and brushed a kiss across her lips. "Hey, beautiful. Ready?"

"I just need to grab my bag and jacket. Have a seat and I'll be right back." She hurried back to her bedroom and put the buds in their case before gathering up everything. When she returned, he was standing in the same spot.

He eased the duffle from her hand and led her down to his car. After they were settled, instead of starting the engine he shifted to face her. "We have to make a quick stop first."

Something in his expression gave her pause. "Okay," she said slowly. "Is there a problem?"

"No. My mother asked, no *demanded* I bring you over so she can meet you."

Jayana wished she knew what he was thinking, but his expression gave away nothing. "Do you have a problem with me meeting her? It might be a little too soon for meet-the-parents, but no way am I going to get on her bad side by declining her...um...demand. So start this baby up and let's get this party started."

Dante shook his head. "I'm almost afraid for the two of you to meet," he muttered.

She stared out the window and tried not to be hurt by his statement. "Why? If you don't want me to meet her, fine."

He turned her face toward him. "Whatever you're thinking, that's not it, baby."

Baby? The endearment made her pulse skip.

"What I meant is that you two are a lot alike and the both of you together are going to give me fits. Trust me when I tell you my mother is going to love you."

"Oh. That makes me feel better." Jayana wanted to ask what he meant by them giving him fits, but she decided to wait and see how the visit went first. They passed the drive talking about everything from their favorite music artists—they both loved her Atlanta hometown girl, Zena Fuller—to best vacation spots. Any calm she felt fled the moment he parked in his mother's circular driveway in the upscale neighborhood. Because he'd said to dress casual, she had on a pair of jeans, a V-neck tee and ballet flats. Had she known she'd be meeting his mother, and in what looked like a mini-mansion, she would've opted for something dressier, or at least business casual. He helped her out of the car, but didn't let go of her hand.

Dante placed a kiss on her temple. "Relax. I can feel the tension bouncing off you."

"Hey, I haven't been introduced to anybody's mama since my high school prom, so I'm a little nervous."

Gathering her in his embrace, he said, "Again, you have nothing to worry about. I promise."

"I'm holding you to it. If she doesn't like me, I'm gonna seriously hurt you, Dante Powell." His rumbling laughter vibrated against her cheek. She backed out of his arms. He stuck his key in the door, but before he could turn the lock, it swung open. A beautiful, trim woman a couple of inches shorter than her stood in the doorway with a wide smile. She had the same toffee coloring as Dante with salt and pepper hair that hung straight around her shoulders.

"It's about time you got here. You must be Jayana. Please come in." She took Jayana's hand and pulled her into the house, then turned back. "You coming in, son?"

"I guess. Can't even get a hello and I'm supposed to be your favorite son."

His mother waved a dismissive hand. "Just close the door and hush. See what I have to deal with," she said to Jayana.

"I'm just going to be the guest for today. I'll take sides next time."

Mrs. Powell laughed. "Dante, she's definitely a keeper. Can I get you anything? If you haven't had lunch, I can fix something."

"Ah, Mom, we have lunch plans already. We just stopped by so you can meet her."

"Oh, okay."

Jayana bit her lip to hide her smile at the woman's disappointment. "I'm sure we have a few minutes to talk, though. Right, Dante?"

He nodded.

They followed Mrs. Powell through an elegantly decorated living room to the family room and sat. The entire house could have been featured in one of those home magazines.

"I understand from my daughter that you two met on a flight, then you ended up working at the center."

"Yes, and we were both surprised." Jayana hazarded a glance at Dante, hoping his mother didn't know the details of that first "meeting."

"I bet, but I've heard a lot of good things about you and how you're already making a difference in those children's lives."

"I hope so. It's a great place to work and I really enjoy the students." Mrs. Powell launched into an interrogation about where Jayana previously lived and worked, where she saw herself in five years, and threw out not-so-subtle hints about her hopes for Jayana and Dante's relationship.

About five minutes in, Dante said, "Okay, Mom. We need to get going. You've grilled her long enough."

Mrs. Powell brought a hand to her chest and said innocently, "I don't know what you're talking about. We're just having a simple conversation."

"Mmm hmm. If that's what you want to call it." He extended his hand and gently pulled Jayana to her feet, then did the same with his mother.

Jayana enjoyed the mother-son interaction. Although, he'd cut her off, both were smiling and she could sense the deep love and affection they shared. She'd missed having the same, being so far away from her own parents. "It was so nice to meet you, Mrs. Powell."

"Same here, Jayana. Next time, you can join us for our family dinner. I'll let Dante know the date and time in advance."

She didn't know how to answer that, so she settled for a smile and a nod. Clearly his mother was in matchmaking mode. After a quick round of goodbyes, Dante hustled them out the door and into the car. "I like your mom."

"And she liked you, if you couldn't tell," he said as he pulled off.

"I felt like I should've been sworn in on the witness stand the way she fired those questions at me. Has she always been this intense with women you'd dated?" Her parents, particularly her father, had done the same with her ex-boyfriend, and neither of them had been impressed. In fact, her mother almost cheered when Jayana ended the relationship.

Dante slanted her a glance. "You're the first woman she's met in four years and the only one she's questioned that way."

She smiled at that thought and focused her attention on the passing scenery. "Where are we going for lunch?" she asked a few minutes later.

"You'll see."

Jayana waited for him to elaborate, but he said nothing. Deciding to go with the flow, she made herself comfortable in the soft-as-butter leather seats and bobbed her head to the music as he merged into traffic. LA, she was learning had about as much traffic as Atlanta, even on the weekends. A while later, he parked in a lot behind an old building with a sign that read, Burger Palace. The neighborhood was a little run down, but the smells wafting from the place made her stomach growl.

"I promised you burgers and pastramis, and this place has the best of both."

That he remembered made her fall a little harder. She

threw her arms around him. "Thank you for this." She rubbed her hands together with glee. "I am so ready." It only took her a minute to decide on the pastrami. He ordered the same. "How long have you been coming here?"

"Since I was a kid. My parents loved the place and I looked forward to them bringing us on some weekends."

It only took a few minutes for the food to be ready. When Dante brought the tray to the table, just one look told her it was going to be good. "Look at all this meat." It had to be a good two inches high, and had extra mustard and pickles the way she liked. Jayana bit into the juicy sandwich and nearly swooned. She hummed and danced in her seat because it was *that* good.

"Does that mean you're enjoying it?" Dante asked with a chuckle.

"I'm over here acting like a kid at Christmas. What do you think? You get big points for this." If the rest of the day went like this, she'd be in love with him by sunset.

CHAPTER 6

"*I*'m going to save this for my lunch on Monday," Jayana said as they got back into the car. She had only eaten half of her pastrami sandwich. Dante, on the other hand, demolished the entire thing with no problem. "Where to next?"

"We have a good half an hour drive to our next stop, so you can kick back and relax."

"That's all you're going to say?"

"Yep."

"Okay, Mr. Keeping Secrets. Be that way."

He gave her the smile that always made her heart beat a little faster. "I will."

"That's fine. I don't need to know." She said the words, but her curiosity called her a liar. Since he'd apparently said all he planned to on the subject, she did as he suggested. Jayana reclined her seat some and closed her eyes.

"Wake up, sleepyhead."

"What?" She groaned and rolled her head in his direction. "Did I fall asleep on you? Sorry." She sat up and covered a yawn. "Where are we?"

Dante pointed in front of them.

"The beach!" *He's really going to make me love him.* She jumped out of the car before he could get out and come around. He gave her a look. "Oops, sorry. Your chivalry still stands. I'm just excited."

"You mentioned walking on the beach being one of your favorite things. It's mine too, so I figured we could do it together."

He held out his hand, entwined their fingers and started a slow stroll down to the water's edge. Jayana inhaled the salty air and exhaled slowly. They stopped every now and again to watch the waves crashing against the shore, then continued. She didn't know how long they walked before reversing their course and heading back to the car. They took a few minutes to empty the sand out of their shoes first. "This has been the best date I've had in a long while. I'm really enjoying myself." She didn't mind the whole wining and dining thing, but she preferred simple moments like this.

"I'm glad." Dante slid his arm around her, lowered his head and captured her lips in a tender kiss. "It's been the best date for me, too."

He kissed her one last time, then held the car door open and waited for her to get in. So many emotions swirled inside of Jayana. Her head kept telling her it was too soon, but her heart said something completely different. He drove a couple of miles, then turned into the driveway of a two-story home in a Manhattan Beach neighborhood with stately homes and manicured lawns. "This is your house? It's gorgeous."

"Thanks." He led her up the walkway, unlocked the door and moved back for her to enter first.

Jayana stepped into a wide foyer that opened into a huge living room. Her footsteps echoed on the highly polished wood floors. The open floor plan was flooded with natural light and she zeroed in on the beautiful black piano on the far side. He had an expansive kitchen with a breakfast bar and two islands, and a sliding glass door that led to an outdoor patio. On the other side sat a family room with dark leather furniture. She knew, instinctively, that he spent a lot of time there. "I love this place. How long have you lived here?"

"Five years."

"I want to see the rest of the house, but first, you promised to play the piano for me." She hooked her arm in his and nearly dragged him back to the living room.

Dante slid onto the bench and pressed a few keys. "What do you want to hear?"

She shrugged. "Whatever your fingers play." When he mentioned playing the piano, she figured it had been a hobby of sorts, but from the first slow jazzy note, the man played as if he should be on a stage headlining somewhere. She stood transfixed as he played. One song ended and he started another, this one mid-tempo. When it ended, she had tears in her eyes.

"What is it, sweetheart?"

Jayana was so overcome with emotion, she could barely speak. "You are amazing. What were you playing?"

"Both pieces are by Ramsey Lewis. The first one was 'Love's Serenade' and the second was 'A Night in Bahia.'" My mom loves his music, so I learned to play quite a few of his songs."

She reached up and touched his face. "You are truly gifted, Dante." Unable to find the words for how his music made her feel, she let her kiss say it all. What started as soft and sweet turned hot and all-consuming in a nanosecond. She didn't know who moved first, but their clothes went flying and they ended up with him sitting on the piano bench while she straddled his lap.

"Hold up," Dante said, his breathing as ragged as hers. He reached down for his discarded pants, grabbed a condom out of his wallet and quickly sheathed himself.

Before she could draw her next breath, he gripped her hips and brought slowly down on his thick erection. Jayana moaned as he filled her completely. Never leaving his gaze, she lifted off him, then eased back down, swirling her hips in a figure eight motion. She repeated the motion a few more times until he increased the pace, moving with deep, steady thrusts. Their blended cries sounded in the room and she dug her nails into his muscular shoulders, holding on for the exquisite ride he was giving her. *"Mmm."*

"I can't get enough of you." He let out a low growl, his strokes coming faster and faster.

Jayana threw her head back as her body trembled with pleasure unlike anything she'd ever felt. He latched on to an erect nipple, sucking, teasing, and making her cry out again.

"Come for me, baby," he whispered, then slanted his mouth over hers, mimicking the movements of his lower body.

She tore her mouth away, her back arched as the pressure built inside her. He cupped her bare bottom and drove his shaft deeper and faster until she climaxed all around him, screaming his name. *"Dante!"* A moment later, he yelled out her name, shuddering as he came. Jayana dropped her head on his shoulder, her body boneless and completely satisfied. Dante's arms tightened around her and they stayed that way for the longest time. She lifted her head and he crushed his mouth against hers in a deep, passionate kiss infused with something she couldn't identify.

"I can't move."

"Me either," she said with a soft moan. Her eyelids grew heavy and she started to drift off. "I love you." *What did I just say?* Her eyes popped open and she muttered a curse, but she didn't move a muscle. Neither did Dante. When he didn't say anything, she released the breath she'd been holding and relaxed, but only marginally. Had she meant it? Yes. Had she meant to say it out loud...and *now*? Hell no! Was she going to address it? Absolutely not. *Please don't let me have scared the man off.*

Dante reread the same page for the fourth time, then tossed the paper aside. Every time he started, his thoughts would drift to Jayana's soft confession. *I love you.* He had no idea if she'd meant it or if she'd blurted it out because the sex had been amazing. He also had no clue whether she hadn't brought it up again because he never reciprocated. It had caught him by surprise and he didn't respond because the words had gotten stuck in his throat. Three simple words, that carried a weight that could never be described as simple. Though he and Jayana had gone to lunch earlier in the week, neither had brought it up. The easy camaraderie they'd always shared had disappeared, leaving in its wake wariness and uncertainty. They would have to deal with it sometime soon, but right now, he had to get through this document.

Picking up the sheet again, he began again. His tech company was working to develop an infinity battery that could be installed into any battery-operated device, and would continuously recharge when near their wireless power transmitter. He managed to read the first two paragraphs and he heard a knock. Dante had purposely closed the door to minimize interruptions. Sighing, he set the document aside and called, "Come in."

"Hey, big brother." Erika strode in and sat. "You busy?"

"Going over the information related to the infinity battery."

"Oh. Then I won't keep you long. And it's a great idea, by the way. I'll get right to it. You need to fix whatever is wrong between you and Jayana."

He groaned inwardly. "Who said there was anything wrong?"

She rolled her eyes. "Please. You don't think I've noticed you going back to your old smile-once-a-week self? She loves you, you love her, and that scares the crap out of you. And for what? Something you had no control over."

"Erika." He didn't have time for this today.

"I know you're the older brother, but today, you're going to sit and listen to me," she said, pointing a finger his way. Her voice softened. "We all know you blame yourself for Dad's death, but that's not on you, Dante. There's no way we'll ever know if the outcome would have been different."

He buried his head in his hands. The weight of the memory pressed down on his chest like a two-ton boulder. "It is my fault. I should've called a nursing service instead of leaving Danielle there with him." Dante's gaze shifted to the picture of him and his father taken at a fundraiser, a face so reminiscent of his own and he felt the memories rising. He should still be here and not lying in a cold grave. Even after four years, the pain of losing his hero remained. Briefly closing his eyes, he swallowed the lump and fought to control his emotions.

"No," Erika said firmly. "It's not. This is all on her. Danielle is a selfish bitch! I knew it, Mom knew it, and so did Ryan. Oh, she played the game well, but the moment you slid that engagement ring on her finger, she flipped the switch and her true self came out. And I let her know just how I felt when I saw her coming out of Sephora at South Bay Galleria two months ago."

Dante's head came up sharply and he frowned. "Wait,

wait. What?" His little spitfire sister didn't play when it came to family and he didn't even want to know what she'd said.

Her eyes narrowed. "She had the nerve to introduce me to her two hussy friends, then said to tell you to call her sometime because you were good together and she didn't understand why you haven't taken her calls, since you obviously hadn't dated anyone else. So, I knocked her on her pompous, silicone ass and told her she'd better be glad I left her breathing, which is more than she had done." Erika fanned herself. "I'm getting heated just thinking about it. But that's water under the bridge. We're talking about the here and now. Let the guilt go and be happy. Talk to Jay. I know she'll understand. Better yet, you should just make an appointment with her and stretch out on that fancy sofa you bought for her office," she added with a smirk.

He was still stuck on her hitting Danielle and it took a minute for his brain to catch up. "Erica—"

"Just do it. I don't want to see you moping around next weekend when all the festivities are going on. By the way, I love the names you came up with for each party." They'd decided on Blocked in Black for the block party and Journey Forward for the gala. She stood and started for the door. "Mom loves Jayana and I want her to be my new big sister, so get it together and fix your life. You can't be rolling solo to your own party."

Still trying to process how she changed subjects on a dime, he asked, "And what about you bringing a date?"

Erika grinned. "I have a sexy, handsome date."

Dante jumped to his feet. "Hold up. Just who is this guy, and why haven't I met him?"

"You've known him most of your life."

It took a moment for him to realize who she meant. *"Ryan? You're dating Ryan?"*

"Yep, and before you go all scary-big-brother, remember you told me you trusted him with your life and mine."

She would choose to remind him of that *now*. However, he hadn't meant romantically. And if he really had to choose a man for her, Ryan would top the list, but still she was his baby sister.

"It sort of just happened...kind of like you and Jayana." She shrugged. "So we decided to see where it goes. It was a little weird at first because I'd always thought of him as another big brother, but a couple of his kisses cured me of that...*quickly*." Erika wiggled her eyebrows. "Who knows? If you get yourself together, we can have a double wedding."

Dante held up a hand. "Okay, you know what...just go. I can't have this conversation with you right now." The thought of her kissing any man, as irrational as it seemed, didn't sit well with him.

Laughing, she said, "See you later, and go talk to Jayana. It's time for you to lay those demons to rest."

Still reeling from the entire conversation, he dropped back down in his chair. Erika was right, though. He needed to talk to Jayana and explain everything, then maybe he could lay his demons to rest. *And tell her I love her.*

CHAPTER 7

"*G*irl, will you look at this," Karina said.

Jayana scanned the crowded park, where hundreds of people had gathered for the Blocked in Black Fest. "It's mind-blowing. I didn't think this many people would show up." The house-front façades behind the vendor booths really gave the feeling of an old fashion block party. A DJ had been positioned at one end of the "block" and a stage for the musical headliner, who would perform later, at the other. She and Karina meandered through the space, stopping to chat with people who sold everything from handmade jewelry, purses and clothing, to hair care, books, all mediums of art, and spa goods and services. A smaller section had been set up for children, and delicious smells from the food court made her mouth water. And every business was Black-owned.

"I've lived here a year and had no idea there were so many Black Businesses. I've been collecting cards, so I can shop and pass them along."

"I hear you. It's all about recycling our Black dollars." The two women exchanged a high-five. Jayana spotted Erika with a group of children and waved.

"Who are you waving at?"

"Dante's sister."

"Speaking of Dante, are you two still circling around each other?"

She accepted the small sample of homemade ice cream from a woman and thanked her before answering. "I don't know if circling is the right word. He still calls, we had lunch in his office last week, but something is still off." Ever since her mouth slid past her brain and uttered those three little words, Dante seemed to be backing away, but not enough to say they'd broken up. The kisses they'd shared when he walked her to her car yesterday definitely didn't fall into the category of we're-not-together-anymore.

"I hope you guys can talk soon. I caught a glimpse of him talking to another fine brother, and I can't wait to meet them both."

Jayana laughed. Karina was just as outspoken and she, and, together, they had been trouble for the guys trying to run a game on them. "If you're talking about Ryan, I don't think he's available." A couple of weeks ago, she'd been coming from the bathroom and caught him and Erika kissing. They didn't see her and she hadn't mentioned it. *Sort of like what you're doing with Dante*, her annoying inner voice said. Like she needed any reminders. Dante appeared and started in their direction. His confident stroll and drop-dead fine face had women stopping to stare, and she was no different. He smiled at her and her heart started pounding. The intense look in his eyes had her searching for a vacant building where they could indulge in another round of *right now* because she wanted him. Now and later. Someone called out to him and he gave her a look of regret, then followed the man. "I thought I would be able to introduce you, but someone just snagged his attention."

"Again. Well, we might as well go find some food."

"I'm down with that." On the way, she saw a few of her students and they hugged her and introduced their parents. Their encouraging words and gratitude warmed her heart, and she hoped she'd always be able to make a positive impact in theirs and other student's lives. She and Karina ended up sharing a plate of fried chicken wings.

"Oh, my goodness. This is so good," Karina said around a mouthful. "I'm going back and get more to take home before they close." She ate and did a little dance to the music being played.

"Hey, baby."

Jayana spun around and almost dropped her wing. "Dante. You scared the crap out of me."

"Sorry." Dante kissed her.

"I want you to meet my best friend and partner in crime, Karina Hall. Rina, this is Dante Powell."

"It's nice to finally meet you, Dante," Karina said. "I would shake your hand, but chicken grease on the first introduction ain't a good look."

He laughed. "Nice meeting you, too. I see why you two are friends, and I can imagine all the trouble you cause."

Jayana bumped him playfully. "Whatever. This turned out so good," she said, waving her hand around. "You should be proud. And the Black history booth has been crowded since I got here." Dante had created a mini museum-like area that had information on LA's Black history and the significance of Juneteenth.

He glanced around. "I'm glad everyone seems to be having a good time."

"I agree. Oh, and thanks for the invite to the Journey Forward Gala tomorrow night," Karina said. "You wouldn't happen to have any single friends who're looking for a date? And only the ones who aren't crazy."

"None that come to mind," Dante said with a laugh. "Do you mind if I steal Jayana away for a few minutes?"

"Not at all. Just don't sneak off to find a place to make out." She laughed when Jayana skewered her with a look. "I'm just sayin'."

Jayana's mouth fell open. "You know I can't stand you right now. Go eat your chicken, crazy woman. I'll be back." As she and Dante walked away, she said, "Can't take her nowhere." After finishing her wing, she wiped her hands on the wet napkin she'd been given and tossed both into a trashcan they passed. She took a few sips from the bottle of water in her tote, then popped a mint into her mouth. "Where are we going?"

"There's someone I want you to meet." She started to ask who, but figured he'd give her the same *you'll see* answer he always did when he wanted to surprise her, so she stifled the urge.

"Yo, Mr. Powell." They turned to see Travis waving at them. "I see you, and Ms. Cole." He flashed a wide grin and gave them the thumbs up.

She and Dante looked at each other and burst out laughing. Jayana said, "Gotta love these kids." Dante led her to a building in a restricted area. Obviously, the security guard recognized Dante because he let them in without a word. The suspense was killing her. They rounded a corner and stopped at a closed door. He knocked a couple of times and the door was opened by a man who looked vaguely familiar. Recognition dawned and her hands went to her mouth. "Oh, my goodness. You're Donovan Wright. Monte's manager," she squealed.

Donovan chuckled. "I am. You must be Jayana. Nice to meet you."

"Same here." She heard soft laughter, forgot all her home training, and went straight into fangirl mode. "*Zena!*"

Smiling, Zena Fuller spread her arms. "Yep, it's me."

Jayana launched herself at Dante, almost knocking him over. "Thank you, thank you! Oh, I need to get a picture. I *love* your music, and I'm from Atlanta, too." *Calm down, girl. You're a professional.* She took a deep breath and tried to get herself in control. She whipped out her phone. "Dante, can you take our picture? Oh, wait." She waved her hands around. "I'm so sorry. Let me get myself together and act like I have some sense. Um, Zena, would it be okay if we took a picture together?"

"Hey, anything for a fellow sister from the ATL."

She handed her phone to Dante and went to stand next to Zena. He took a few shots, then had her check them to see if they were to her liking. "These are great. Thanks, baby." Facing Zena, she said, "Thank you so much for your graciousness. I've been a fan of yours since you hit the scene and I am *so* happy to see you finally getting the notoriety you deserve."

"Thank you so much for saying that, and for supporting me all these years. And I am grateful for the opportunity to do what I love. My incredible husband hooked me up with the best manager and record company and the ride has been nothing short of amazing."

They shared one last hug, then Jayana and Dante left her to get ready. The show would start in fifteen minutes. "That was the best surprise *ever*. Thank you," she said to Dante as they headed back down the hallway. He stopped abruptly and pulled her into another empty room. "What are you doing?" she asked, laughing. Karina's last statement flashed in her mind.

"We need to talk." He closed the door behind them and gestured for her to sit.

Her smile faded. "Oh." Was he planning to break things off?

Dante took the chair next to her and bowed his head, but didn't speak for several seconds.

Jayana's heart rate sped up. When he lifted his head, misery was reflected in his eyes. "Dante?"

He grasped her hand. "I owe you an apology, Jayana. I know I haven't been present in this relationship like I should have."

"If this is about me saying I love you—"

He cut her off with a kiss. "It is and it isn't." Blowing out a long breath, he stroked his beard.

He seemed to be having a difficult time with whatever he planned to say. The woman who loved him wanted to shout, "Just tell me!" The professional in her said to wait quietly until he was ready to speak. She chose the latter, giving his hand a gentle squeeze of encouragement.

Finally, he spoke. "Four years ago, I was engaged to be married."

Oo-kay. That's not what she expected to hear, but held the thousand and one questions she wanted to ask.

"In the month following our engagement, my ex-fiancée began to turn into someone I didn't recognize. Everything was about her and what she wanted, and I'd started to have second thoughts. During that the same time, my father had a heart attack and was hospitalized for almost two weeks. When he came home, my sister and I took turns helping Mom manage his care." He paused, as if gathering his next thoughts.

Dread crept up Jayana's spine, and she tightened her grip on his hand. She could feel the anxiety and anger bouncing off him in waves.

"Mom had to fly out of town for a two-day conference. She didn't want to go, but my dad insisted. I promised I'd stay over and take care of him because Erika had gone out of town for training with her job. This was a year or so before we opened the youth center," he added. "Everything was fine until I asked Danielle to hang out with my father while I went to pick up my mother from the airport. Her flight was on time, but another plane was at their gate and they had to sit on the runway for a few minutes. I called Danielle to let her know I'd be about ten or fifteen minutes later than I thought." Dante stood up and paced, then stopped. "She said that marrying me didn't include babysitting an old man, and she had plans with her friends to go shopping for a wedding dress."

Jayana gasped softly and felt her own anger rising. "You have got to be freakin' kidding me. Shopping for a damn dress? She acted like you asked her to provide twenty-four hour care for a week. *Ugh!*"

"When my mother and I got there, she was gone. I guess she'd called someone to pick her up. But my father..." He hesitated, seemingly trying to control his emotions, then sat again. "We found him in the middle of the bedroom floor clutching his phone. He was trying to call me, but he was gone," he said in an anguished whisper. "I trusted her."

His voice cracked and tears ran down her cheeks. Now she understood. "You blamed yourself." And because she broke his trust, that same mistrust and unwillingness to open himself up again had been passed down to every other woman who came behind her.

Dante nodded. "If I had just—"

Jayana left her chair, hunkered down in front of him and cupped his face between her hands. "Listen to me, Dante. I can't even imagine the kind of pain you must have felt that day, and I'm not going to try. The guilt must be eating you up inside, but you are not to blame for her selfishness, sweetheart." She had to clamp her jaws shut for a minute to keep from saying something to make it worse, like asking where the heffa lived so she could beat her ass. "I know you're afraid to love me because of what she did, but had it been me, I would've never left your father's side. The love I have for you would have been extended to him and I would have cared for him as if he were my own father." The tears standing in his eyes made hers come faster. "Let go of the pain and guilt, Dante, and let me love you the way she should have loved you. The way I already love you. Trust me with your love, with your heart. I promise to take good care of it."

Dante crushed her to him. "I love you, Jayana. So much."

Hearing him say the words filled her heart to near bursting. *I will love you always.*

CHAPTER 8

"Freedom and true equality gives us the opportunity to be seen and celebrated beyond the color of our skin," Dante said to the students and families gathered at the gala Sunday evening. "As we continue to learn from the past and strive toward creating a better future, we have to be committed to increasing equity and eradicating racial injustice in the Black community. Don't settle for mediocrity. Set your sights on something higher and don't let anyone tell you what you can't do. I want you soar, to journey forward, then reach back and help those coming behind you." He stepped away from the podium to thunderous applause, stopping to shake hands and accept hugs.

"Nice speech. Short and to the point, as always," Ryan said, meeting Dante halfway and handing him a glass filled with an amber liquid.

"Thanks."

"Man, this was a brilliant idea. Look at their faces. I don't think I've ever seen these kids smile so much."

He took a sip, recognizing it as an old fashion, his drink

of choice. "I know. I'm going to make this an annual function." His Mr. Black duties would end in three years, but this
was his legacy. During the tour of the museum, many of the
students had shared that they never knew their history. It
was up to all of them to make sure they never forgotten.

"So, why didn't you tell me about you and Erika?" Dante
asked, changing the subject.

"Honestly, I didn't know how you'd feel about it."

He still didn't know how he felt about it. "I love you like a
brother, but she *is* my baby sister. If you hurt her, I will kick
your ass."

"You know me, D. And I would never hurt Erika. To hurt
her would be like hurting myself."

Like how he felt about Jayana. He had to give it to Erika.
She'd been right about him baring his soul to Jayana. Their
conversation yesterday had been cathartic, healing. Dante
was honest with himself and knew he still had some things to
work out, and was even contemplating scheduling a few
sessions with someone to talk. "If I had to pick a guy for her
—and I'm still not saying I would—you'd get my vote." He
held out his fist and Ryan tapped his lightly against it.

"Now that I'm off the hot seat, what's up with you and
Jayana?"

"I told her everything."

Ryan choked on his drink. Coughing, he pounded on his
chest a few times to clear his throat. "I'm glad because she
really loves you, but I never thought you would." He lifted a
brow. "Y'all good now?"

"We are. I am." He said the words to his friend, but his
gaze was locked on the beautiful woman who owned his
heart. Jayana stood across the room talking and laughing
with a couple of the students. The black one-shoulder gown
wrapped over the side of her neck and down to one long
sleeve, and left the other arm and her upper back bare. It

skimmed every one of her curves and had a side slit that ended mid-thigh. He'd been in a state of arousal from the moment she opened the door to him.

"About damn time. She's good people, Dante. Don't let her get away."

"I don't plan to."

"I'm going to dance with my woman. You should do the same."

On the heels of his departure, Dante's mother approached. He bent to kiss her cheek. "You look beautiful, as always, Mom." The elegant long-sleeved, pale gold gown draped elegantly over her trim figure and made her look like a queen.

"Thank you, honey. You outdid yourself with this event, both events, and I'm so proud of you. Your dad would be too."

"That means a lot, so thank you," he said around the lump in his throat.

"Jayana is such a wonderful young woman."

"She is."

"There are a lot of women who are eager to stand at your side." She glanced up at him. "Like Danielle. But none of them have ever been truly *on* your side. Not like Jayana. So many people never get to experience real love, the kind I had with your father," she added with a wistful smile. "Don't be one of them, son. You've been blessed with another chance, so grab hold of it."

"I hear you, Mom. And if you'll excuse me, I'm going to do just that." Dante kissed her cheek and went to claim his woman. Jayana saw him, excused herself and met him halfway.

"Ooh, you look so good tonight in this tux that I want to drag you into a closet somewhere...*right now*."

He chuckled. She took every opportunity to throw that

phrase in his face, but he wasn't mad. Each time, it ended with them naked and him buried deep inside her. "How about we settle for a dance, then I'll see what I can do about the rest later because I definitely want to slowly strip that dress off you and taste every inch of your beautiful body."

"Works for me, but if you keep talking like that, we aren't going to make it to the dance floor. So, come on. One of us has to behave."

Laughing, Dante led her onto the floor where the band was playing a slow, jazzy number and gathered her in his embrace. She rested her head against his shoulder as they started a slow sway. He could stand here holding her in just this way for the rest of his life. "Have I told you how much I love you?" he whispered close to her ear.

"You may have mentioned it once or twice," she said, lifting her head. "But feel free to tell me again."

"I love you, baby." Without thinking, he lowered his head and covered her mouth in a passionate kiss, swirling his tongue around hers, and letting her sweetness seep into his soul. He got so lost in her taste that it took a moment for the applause to register. Dante broke off the kiss and saw that he and Jayana were the only two people on the dance floor, while everyone around them clapped and whistled.

"Well, if anybody didn't know we're dating, they know now," Jayana said, direct as usual.

And he didn't have one problem with it. In fact, he wanted to shout it to the world.

"Everybody not on the bus in the next ten minutes is going to be left behind," Dante called out to the excited teenagers. He did a few field trips during the summer—some educational, some for fun. Today's trip to the beach would be strictly fun.

The twenty-five students rushed over, all clamoring to get on first.

"Nothing like a good you're-gonna-get-left speech to get them moving," Jayana said as she passed him carrying a box. "They'd better not hold me up from getting to my beloved sand and ocean."

He smiled. His baby loved the beach and with the warm July temperatures, they made a trip there at least once a week, sometimes two. The last three months with her had been amazing and he'd do anything to keep her happy. Dante had worked through his issues with a therapist and it had been the best thing for him and their relationship. Mental health at the center had always been a priority, but now he planned to work harder to help erase the stigma tied to Black men and therapy. He wanted the young men at the center to know that seeking help when needed didn't make them weak.

Minutes later, after checking and double-checking that everyone was onboard and accounted for, the bus pulled off. The teens spent the twenty-minute drive to Santa Monica Pier singing, laughing and telling jokes. When they arrived, Dante stood to give some instructions. "You'll need to remain with your group and your chaperone at all times. They are in charge. You are not. Anyone who's caught violating the rules will return to the bus until it's time to leave." He peeked at his watch. "It's eleven-thirty now, and we'll meet back here at the bus for lunch at one-thirty. Any questions?" No one spoke. "Okay, let's go have some fun." Because they had more chaperones than needed, it freed him up to check on all the groups and be available for any mishaps.

The kids walked along the pier, splashed in the water and chased each other in the sand. Dante smiled at Jayana sitting in the sand with three of the younger teens building a sand castle. "Are you having fun?" he asked her.

"We are. You should join us."

He couldn't recall the last time he'd played in the sand, but he joined the group as they used the buckets and shovels the center provided to dig paths, create walls and carve out windows in the wet sand.

"Mr. Powell, I want to come to this center forever," one twelve-year-old girl stated.

"You know we only go up to age eighteen. After that, you'll be going to college. Do you know what you want to study?"

She nodded excitedly. "I want to be an engineer like you."

That she wanted to follow in his footsteps filled him with pride. He and Jayana shared a smile. "I'm honored, and I'm going to do all I can to help your achieve that goal." He had already started working on ways to offer summer internships to juniors and seniors in high school at InstaGenix, and had reached out to a couple of buddies who headed Black-owned companies to do the same.

After a short while longer, Dante left to check on the other groups. He had to step in to resolve a mild disagreement between two students, but found no other fires to put out.

A few minutes before lunch, he sent a text to Ryan, asking him to meet at the bus so they could begin the preparations. They planned to take their picnic down to the beach and he had already asked Erika and another parent to save the spot. The two women laid out enough blankets for everyone to have room without being crowded.

Ryan pulled out his phone. "I'm going to send a reminder text to the chaperones to make their way over here."

"Sounds good," Dante said, hauling coolers from under the

bus's storage area. The groups drifted over and assisted with the transport of food and drinks. Once everyone settled down, they stuffed themselves on an assortment of sandwiches, chips, fruit and homemade cookies prepared by one of the parents. He synced his phone to the large Bluetooth speaker he'd brought, selected a playlist of popular songs and cranked up the music.

They laughed at the students engaging in a dance contest.

"I wish I would try some of those moves," one parent said, shaking her head. "I don't know how these children bend their bodies like that. You'd have to carry me out of here on a stretcher. I've gone far beyond dropping it like it's hot. I can't even let it down like it's warm anymore. I'm at the stage where I'm easing it down like it's room temperature."

Dante almost choked on a cookie laughing so hard.

She pointed a finger his way. "Keep living, Dante. One day you're going to wake up with aches and pains in places you didn't even know ached."

He held up his hands in mock surrender. "I'm getting close." He used to be able to get up at least three feet off the ground when he played basketball. Now, he was lucky if he got eighteen inches.

The laughter continued and dancing continued, then it was time to clean up. "Jayana, can you come to the bus and help me get the special treat I have?" Dante asked, standing.

"Of course." She accepted his help up and they trudged through the sand once more. "My thighs are getting a good workout walking back and forth in this sand."

"I'll be more than happy to give you a good massage."

Jayana grinned up at him. "You ain't said nothing but a word."

Chuckling, he slung an arm around her shoulders and kissed her temple. In the bus, he retrieved the three dozen cupcakes decorated in blue and purple frosting and they carried them back.

"They're decorated so pretty, and you know these are my favorite colors." Her steps slowed when the neared the group. "What is—?"

Erika and Ryan rushed over to relieve them of the dessert.

Dante took Jayana's hand and walked her over to a heart-shaped design done with red rose petals and stood in the middle. He dropped to one knee.

"I can't believe you're gonna have me out here doing the ugly cry in front of all these people, but go ahead." Chuckles sounded in the group.

He loved this woman. "Jayana, from the first day we met, I knew you were special, even if I couldn't see how you'd fit into my life. But my eyes are wide open now and there will never be another woman for me. You are the only one I will ever love and I want to spend the rest of my life with you. Will you marry me?"

"Yes, yes!" she cried, bouncing up and down. "I love you."

He removed the diamond solitaire from the black velvet box and slid it onto her finger. Before he could stand, she launched herself at him, knocking them both onto the blanket. "I love you, too, sweetheart." She was his right now, his forever, his everything.

EPILOGUE

One year later.

"I'm never letting you touch me again, Dante Powell. Why didn't somebody tell me labor hurt like this? Neither of our mothers said one word."

"If they had, would you have wanted children?" Dante asked, rubbing her back. Both grandmothers had been ecstatic about having their first grandchild. And now with Erika and Ryan's recent marriage, his mother was already campaigning for a second one.

"Hell, no!"

He smiled. "The doctor said it shouldn't be too much longer." She was eight centimeters dilated. "You could always do the epidural." The glare she shot his way would have made a lesser man run out the door. But he was unfazed. She'd been adamant about natural childbirth. He loved his wife to distraction and he now truly understood what his mother meant about real love. However, he didn't know if the crushing grip she had on his hand at the moment could be filed under the same category. He winced, but didn't let go and continued to rub her back. "Breathe, baby. You're almost there."

She let out a loud groan. "I don't know if we have the same definition of almost there. I'm thinking sometime in the next two minutes would be good."

Dante chuckled inwardly. At least she still had her humor.

The nurse came in. "Looks like they're coming a couple of minutes apart now. I'll let the doctor know. Hang in there, Mrs. Powell."

"Mmm hmm, I'm hanging…by a thread."

"I love you, Jayana," he said, shaking his head. The doctor returned and examined her. From that moment, everything seemed to happen in a blur, and forty-five minutes later, their baby girl made her entrance into the world, yelling at the top of her little lungs.

They cleaned her up, weighed and measured her, then wrapped her in a blanket and handed her to Dante. She stopped crying and stared up at him curiously. The sight of his beautiful baby girl put a sheen of tears in his eyes and the immediate love he felt for her nearly overwhelmed him. "Welcome to the world, Carmen Leilani Powell." He placed a gentle kiss on her forehead. "Let's go meet your mama." Dante transferred the precious bundle to Jayana and brushed a kiss across his wife's parched lips. "You did good, sweetheart."

"She's so beautiful." Jayana lifted her hand and Dante placed a kiss on the back. "Okay, I forgive you. I might let you touch me again."

It was never a dull moment with his woman. She was his heart and he'd love her until the end of time.

OTHER BOOKS IN THIS SERIES

ABOUT THE AUTHOR

Sheryl Lister is a multi-award winning author who writes sweet, sensual contemporary romance featuring intelligent and slightly flawed characters who always find love. She is a former pediatric occupational therapist with over twenty years of experience and often says she "played" for a living. A California native, Sheryl is a wife, mother of three daughters and a son-in-love, and grandmother to two special little boys. When she's not writing, Sheryl can be found on a date with her husband or in the kitchen creating appetizers. For more information, visit her website at www.sheryllister.com.

ALSO BY SHERYL LISTER

Her Passionate Promise (Women of Park Manor)

Love's Sweet Kiss (Sassy Seasoned Sisters #1)

Never Letting Go (Carnivale Chronicles)

Embracing Ever After (Once Upon a Baby #1)

Do Me (Irresistible Husband)

Five Midnight Moments (New Year Bae-Solutions)

Tempting Hunter (Once Upon A Funeral #4)

Love's Sweet Surrender (Sassy Seasoned Sisters #2)

Five Mistletoe Moments (Baes of Christmas)

A Table for Two (Firefly Lake #1)

Choose Me (Irresistible Husband)

www.ingramcontent.com/pod-product-compliance
Lightning Source LLC
Chambersburg PA
CBHW071955230626
47052CB00014B/1144